LUST. HATE. LOVE.

ELLA FRANK
BROOKE BLAINE

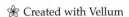

Also by Ella Frank

The Exquisite Series

Exquisite

Entice

Edible

The Temptation Series

Try

Take

Trust

Tease

Tate

True

Confessions Series

Confessions: Robbie

Confessions: Julien

Confessions: Priest

Confessions: The Princess, The Prick & The Priest

Confessions: Henri

Confessions: Bailey

Sunset Cove Series

Finley

Devil's Kiss

Masters Among Monsters Series

Alasdair

Isadora

Thanos

Standalones

Blind Obsession

Veiled Innocence

PresLocke Series

Co-Authored with Brooke Blaine

ACED

LOCKED

WEDLOCKED

Fallen Angel Series

Co-Authored with Brooke Blaine

HALO

VIPER

ANGEL

An Affair In Paris

Co-Authored with Brooke Blaine

Sex Addict

Shiver

Wrapped Up in You

All I Want for Christmas...Is My Sister's Boyfriend

Also by Brooke Blaine

South Haven Series

A Little Bit Like Love

A Little Bit Like Desire

The Unforgettable Duet

Forget Me Not

Remember Me When

L.A. Liaisons Series

Licked

Hooker

P.I.T.A.

Romantic Suspense

Flash Point

PresLocke Series

Co-Authored with Ella Frank

Aced

Locked

Wedlocked

Fallen Angel Series

Co-Authored with Ella Frank

HALO

VIPER

ANGEL

An Affair In Paris

Standalone Novels

Co-Authored with *Ella Frank*

Sex Addict

Shiver

Wrapped Up in You

All I Want for Christmas…Is My Sister's Boyfriend

Prologue

Killian
Six Months Earlier

I TOOK IN a deep drag of my cigarette, and when I exhaled, the smoke formed a cloud that passed over the Atlanta skyline. Tequila buzzed in my veins, courtesy of Halo's sister, Imogen, thrusting shots in my direction all night, quieting the voice in my head that told me what I was thinking was a bad idea.

Instead, I tried to focus on tonight's success and being on top of the world. We'd just killed our first show on the *Corruption* tour, and if that was any indication of how the rest of the dates would go, we'd be flying high for months.

So yeah, I was feeling fucking good. But I *could* be feeling better...

My eyes drifted in the direction of Fallen Angel's new manager. Levi Walker: an enigma wrapped up in a handsome package, one I'd tried not to notice, but lately, I had been failing miserably. It didn't help that I'd noticed him watching me too when he thought I wasn't looking. Charming, self-confident to the point of cocky (which, in this business, you had to be), and so strikingly good-looking that it was no wonder Levi seemed to get whatever he wanted. That was exactly the reason I'd wanted him to take us on as our manager, because he was a guy you didn't say no to, which meant he'd be able to fling open doors for us.

And maybe a small part of why I'd been adamant about him replacing Brian had to do with the way he made my dick hard. Viper and I seemed to have that much in common when it came to new guys.

Levi looked up, his dark eyes meeting mine as I lounged against the wall, taking another inhale of nicotine. Damn, he looked delicious tonight. His blond hair swept across his forehead in the breeze, and he'd pushed up the sleeves of his turquoise button-down shirt, showing off his tanned arms. I'd never thought I had a type until the day I met Levi Walker. One look at him—combined with all that self-confidence—and I knew where this was headed.

He held my gaze until I exhaled, and when the smoke escaped my lips, Levi's eyes dropped to my mouth.

Fuuuck.

My cock throbbed behind my jeans, the way he was watching my mouth making me rock hard in two seconds flat. When his gaze traveled down over my body, I groaned.

God, what the fuck was he waiting for? A sign? My permission? I was pretty sure my entire body was telling him exactly what I wanted, and from the way he wet his lips, I took that as a sign that we were on the same page.

But when Levi's eyes met mine again, there was something unreadable there, and then he looked away, focusing back on the crowd of people around him.

Godfuckingdammit. I was beginning to think I'd have to

spell this shit out for him. But it'd have to be later, because Viper and Halo were headed in my direction.

I bent one of my legs to rest on the back of the wall, hoping to hide my erection, as they came to a stop in front of me.

"Hey," Viper said, his hand encompassing Halo's.

Ah, the lovebirds of Fallen Angel. If I didn't like them so much, and if Halo hadn't simmered Viper to a low boil, I'd probably gag at all the heart-eyes shit. But I couldn't do that, and I found it impossible to resent either of them, not when Viper was happier than I'd ever seen him. And Halo had been good for him *and* for the band.

But right now, they both looked like they'd rather be anywhere but here, celebrating on the roof of the hotel with about a hundred others.

As I looked between the two of them, I smirked. "Lemme guess. You're leaving."

"Aww, whoever said you're just a pretty face?" Viper said.

I brought the cigarette to my lips for another drag and then blew the smoke over my shoulder. "If I'm honest, I'm surprised you both lasted this long. I figured you would've split hours ago."

Viper wrapped an arm around Halo's shoulders and said, "If it'd been up to me—"

Halo whacked a palm on his chest. "I was being sociable."

"*I* was being frustrated," he said.

I laughed, but my eyes caught on Levi for the umpteenth time tonight. He'd moved to the opposite side of the party, chatting it up with a crowd surrounding him and hanging on his every word. I didn't like the way one guy in particular was eyeing Levi like he had plans for them later, but I couldn't think on that for long, because Viper looked in Levi's direction and said, "Something you seem to be familiar with these days."

"Huh?" I reluctantly tore my eyes away from Levi back to where Viper gave me one hell of a smug look.

"Being frustrated. You seem…preoccupied," he said.

I narrowed my eyes. "I'm not preoccupied."

"Could've fooled me," he said. He seemed to be enjoying himself a little too much at my expense. "You can't keep your eyes off our new manager. Not to mention, you didn't invite anyone here tonight. That's *very* unlike you. Thinking about starting some intra-band relations yourself, huh?"

Figured Viper would be the one to pick up on that. I stubbed out my cigarette in one of the ashtrays. "The thought might've crossed my mind."

"Uh huh. I fucking knew it."

I shrugged, not bothering to disagree as I looked back in Levi's direction, and this time, I saw Halo and Viper follow my gaze.

As if he could feel my eyes on him—hell, all our eyes on him—Levi slowly turned in our direction, and when he saw us staring, he narrowed his eyes, as if wondering what mischief we were up to now.

"Act fucking normal," I said under my breath. "I don't want you two to scare him off before I go over there."

Halo, obviously feeling the alcohol tonight, started to laugh. "Oh my God. You and Levi?"

Not that I wanted anyone to know my business, but if the alcohol had gotten to Halo, it'd gotten to me as well, because I was feeling pretty damn good right now—and more than a little ready for some action.

I shot Halo a wink. "If I'm lucky. Now you two get the hell out of here."

Viper had an amused look on his face as he said, "Do I need to tell you not to fuck up a good thing here?"

"I mean, you can," I said, shoving off the wall and looking between Viper and Halo, who had zero room to talk. "But you'll get the same answer you gave me." When Viper arched a brow, I shrugged. "It's none of your damn business."

Viper lifted his hands and backed away as Halo shot me a wide grin and said, "Good luck." Then they were gone, and thank fuck for that. With those two around, I knew Levi would keep one eye on them for any trouble, but with them out of the picture, maybe he'd finally make a move. Or be receptive to mine.

I made my way through the crowd, my eyes zeroing in on Levi. He didn't see me coming; his back was to me, and he was leaning in to a guy who looked too interested, laughing at something Levi was saying.

An irrational flare of jealousy went through me at the move, and as I approached, I stepped between them, cutting off their connection. The smile I gave Levi then was full of a confidence I didn't normally feel to quite this extent—thank you, tequila— and the puzzled look he gave me indicated as much.

"Mind if I steal you away?" I said, and then over my shoulder to what's-his-name, I added, "Band business."

When Levi quickly excused himself, I practically patted myself on the back. Step one, complete.

"Is something wrong?" Levi asked, keeping pace with me as I walked to the far end of the party, where a cluster of private cabanas lined the pool. The area was off-limits to guests at this late hour, but when we approached, one of the security guys lowered the rope without a word. "I saw Viper and Halo talking to you. Did something happen?"

I didn't respond as I chose one of the cabanas facing away from the party for ultimate privacy and made myself comfortable on the large, round sunbed.

"Killian? What's going on?" Levi's forehead creased as he stared down at me, the moonlight lighting him up from behind as if he were standing in a spotlight. I may have been drunk, but I wasn't blind—he was sexy as hell.

I patted the cushion beside me. "Come here and I'll tell you."

Levi eyed me warily but sat. We'd never been anything more than completely professional to each other, so he had no reason to think I would do anything inappropriate now, despite the looks we'd given each other. Even so, I noticed the stiff way he sat, his back straight, his eyes focusing straight ahead.

"What did you want to talk to me about?" he said.

His words came out with an air of caution, so instead of diving right in, I'd ease him into it. *Yeah, good plan...* "Tonight went well, don't you think?"

Levi's eyebrows rose slightly, like he wasn't expecting me to say that and didn't believe that was where I'd been heading. Again, he thought carefully about his words before saying, "You guys played a great first show."

"Thank you." I lay down on my side, propping my head up on my elbow and tracing the patterns on the cushion with my finger. I was aware that the move had my shirt rising enough that he could see how low my jeans sat on my hips, and I watched his eyes roam over my uncovered skin before he swallowed and quickly looked away.

Ahh. So he wasn't completely oblivious to me, was he?

"Did you watch?" I said. Let him think I meant the show when I really meant *me.*

Levi kept his gaze straight ahead. "That's my job, Killian. You guys pay me to watch over you."

I pushed off my elbow to a sitting position and scooted closer to him. "But do you enjoy it? Watching?"

"If I wasn't a fan of the band, I wouldn't have taken this job."

His jaw was set, his whole body tense, like he was holding himself back, and it was that struggle that made me smile. "If you like watching us so much, then why won't you look at me?"

When his breathing grew faster and he still didn't say anything, I took a chance. I laid my hand on his thigh, over the material of his crisp white pants. His eyes shot to mine immediately, and this close I could see the gold flecks in them.

"What are you doing?" he said, his voice coming out in shards of steel, but when he didn't push my hand away, I inched it higher up his thigh and leaned in closer. I could practically taste the citrus on his breath from whatever he'd been drinking tonight.

"I've seen the way you look at me. And I know you've caught me watching you..."

"Like I said. It's my job." Levi's words said one thing, but his body language said another, and when I moved in closer and angled my head slightly, his eyes dropped to my mouth, and that was all it took for my self-control to snap.

My lips were on his in half a heartbeat, but when he froze, I had a moment of panic. Had I gone too far? Had I completely read his signals wrong?

Not wanting to move away and fuck my chance, but not willing to push him further if he didn't want this, I kept my lips lightly grazing his and lifted my free hand to curve along the side of his neck. My touch made Levi shiver, and his eyes squeezed shut as he let out a shaky exhale.

Give in, I thought. *Give in to me...*

I don't think I breathed as I waited to see what he'd do, if he'd meet me halfway. But when he let out a curse, I had my answer.

With a hunger I thought only I'd been feeling, Levi reached for me, his mouth finally parting under mine, allowing me the access I craved. His lips were warm pillows that fit perfectly against mine, and as I dipped my tongue inside his mouth to roam alongside his, I moaned.

Levi clenched his hands in my shirt as he hauled me over the top of him, and my eyes slammed shut as he sucked on my greedy tongue. *Sweet Jesus.* He tasted even better than I thought he would, and when I slid my fingers into his hair to hold his head still, a throaty growl left the man sucking on me like his favorite candy, and I deepened the kiss.

I moved my hand farther up his leg to cup the growing erection I could feel between his thighs, and he groaned into my mouth and arched his hips into my hand—

Levi jerked away suddenly, ripping his mouth free and clamping his hand down on my wrist, shoving it off him. He was breathing hard, his lips swollen and used, his dark eyes conflicted.

"No," he said, gasping for air. "We can't."

"Yes, we can." My cock pounded in time with my heartbeat, and I reached for him again, only to feel him slip out from beneath me. He moved off the bed and got to his feet, a string of curses leaving his mouth.

My head was still spinning from the intensity of his kiss, and I couldn't understand how he'd managed to stop it. "What's the problem?"

Even with his back to me, I could see the way he had to adjust himself before turning to face me.

"Forget this ever happened," he said.

"You expect me to forget a kiss like that? Can you?"

Levi schooled his face into an inscrutable expression, the conflicted look I saw earlier gone. "Yes."

"Why? And don't spout off some bullshit about not wanting this, because clearly you do." I gave a pointed look at his tented pants, and Levi crossed his arms.

"Look, Killian. You're hot. I'm not fucking blind, okay? And yeah, this"—he pointed between us—"would be scorching, because I know exactly what I'd do to a guy like you."

Damn, that sounded promising. "Then come on," I said, spreading my legs in invitation as I gave him a seductive smile. "Don't you wanna have a little fun?"

"No. I don't break my rules. And rule number one is don't

fuck a client. Never have, never will. No matter how tempted I might be."

I leaned back on my hands. "Anyone ever tell you that's a shit-tastic rule?"

"No one's ever had to."

Huh. Was he admitting I was the only one he'd ever been tempted to break his rules for? I could work with that.

"I need to get back to the party, and so do you," Levi said, straightening his shirt and running his hand through his blond hair. With one final look, he walked off, leaving me hot, hard, and still horny as hell in a private cabana meant for two.

I definitely hadn't expected Levi to shut me down tonight, and while part of me felt frustrated by the rebuff, another part of me was waking up to the challenge Levi had just put forth.

He wanted to play by the rules, huh? Well, there was one thing I knew about rules: they were made to be broken.

ONE

Killian

PRESENT DAY

"HELLO? EARTH TO Kill." Viper snapped his fingers in my face, effectively shutting down my thoughts as I blinked him into focus.

Sitting up, I shoved his arm away. "What?"

"You plan on staying here or do you maybe wanna get your ass on the plane?" When he inclined his head toward the open door leading out to the airfield, I realized I was the only one still sitting in the private lounge's club chairs.

With a curse, I rose to my feet and grabbed my bag before following Viper out to where the private plane we'd chartered for our international tour waited. I couldn't tell if I'd fallen asleep or just completely zoned out while we'd been waiting, but either way, I couldn't shake the taste of citrus that lingered on my tongue from the memory of Levi's mouth on mine. God, he'd been fucking delicious, but true to his word, he'd gone back to being mister professional, not so much as looking in my direction.

Well, that was a lie. There was looking, and a whole lot of it, but if he'd been in any way affected by what'd gone on between us after our first night on the *Corruption* tour, he didn't show it.

And didn't that just bust my balls.

"Hey." Viper grabbed my wrist, forcing me to face him. "What the hell's crawled up your ass lately, huh?"

I rolled my eyes and went to turn away, but his grip tightened.

"Or maybe the problem's *nothing* has been up your ass, am I right?" Viper winked, and I finally pulled myself free.

"Go fuck yourself."

"I don't need to. I have Angel."

"Jesus." Running my hand through my hair, I sighed.

"Been a little tense between you and Levi since Atlanta. That the reason for these moods you've been gracing us with?"

"Nope."

Viper narrowed his eyes. "Bullshit. You've gotta get over it, man. Move on."

"I'm over it."

"Really?"

"The fuck do you care?"

"That," he said, pointing at me. "You're not usually such a surly bastard, but you're snapping at everyone—especially Levi."

"So?"

"He shot you down. It happens. Well, not to me, but—"

Crossing my arms over my chest, I glanced up at the waiting jet. "You done?"

"Hmm, let me see..." He laughed. "You know, maybe I should go thank him for knocking your ego down a notch—"

I wrapped my arm around Viper's neck in a headlock and walked us over to the stairs. "That's enough outta you. Keep it zipped."

Laughing, Viper shrugged out of my hold. "If he's not inter-ested, you don't have to be celibate—"

"Oh, he's interested," I said. "He's just playing hard to get."

As Viper snorted, the man in question stuck his head out of the plane and glared our way. "Are you two planning on joining us, or do I have to cancel the Australian leg?"

Damn. Even shooting daggers our way, Levi Walker was a handsome motherfucker. Perfectly manicured scruff lined his strong jaw, and though his hair was dark, he kept the front a white blond that he artfully arranged in a way that showcased how stunning he was. Always put together, always wearing something bold no one else I knew could get away with—today it was a lavender button-up paired with dark purple velvet pants.

"Yeah, he looks like he's interested, all right," Viper whispered before elbowing me in the ribs and heading up the stairs.

As I watched Viper go, my eyes drifted up to Levi, then his focus landed solely on me, and when he noticed I was standing in the exact same spot I had been a second ago, he raised his left eyebrow as if to say, *Get your ass up here, now.*

I sauntered toward the stairs, taking my sweet time, not about to let Levi think he had any say whatsoever when it came to my behavior. But as I got to the top, I stopped and looked him in the eye and realized what a fucking lie that was.

Who am I trying to kid? All my moods lately, which had really just been one—pissy—had been because of this guy, and all because he'd shot me down. Not only shot me down, but shot me down after one of the most spectacular kisses of my life.

"Please, take your time, Killian." Levi looked at the watch circling his wrist and then back to me. "It's not like we're on a tight schedule or anything."

"It's a fucking fourteen-hour flight. Excuse me if I wasn't in a hurry to buckle up and take off."

Levi cocked his head to the side and ran his eyes down over me, and while I usually would've puffed my chest up and tried my hardest to look hot under such a once-over, something in his gaze told me this wasn't that kind of once-over.

"It must be so hard to be you, I know." Levi nodded and pursed his lips. "Buckling up back there with a full bar, big-screen TVs, meals worthy of five-star restaurants, and an actual *bed* if you want it back there. I can understand your less-than-enthusiastic demeanor when it comes to boarding."

Okay, well, when he said it like that, I—

"Killian?"

"Huh? Yeah?"

"Get on the plane before I pull you on it by your hair." The spark in Levi's dark eyes almost made me want to drop my bag down the stairs just to see the firecracker in front of me go off. But then I remembered a story about a kid that held on to one of those damn rockets and got burned really fucking bad, and decided to just get on the damn plane.

That didn't mean I was going to let him have the last say, though. If I had to sit on this plane for fourteen hours staring at Viper and Angel all kissy face and moon-eyed, I at least wanted to know that Levi was thinking about me as much as I was going to be thinking about him.

As I went to brush by Levi, I took a deep inhale and my cock twitched at the intoxicating scent that always accompanied him wherever he went. I had no idea what it was. The name, the brand... Who the hell cared? All I knew was that on Levi it smelled decadent and expensive, like silk sheets and sex, and I wanted to roll around with him naked until our bodies smelled exactly the same.

Unable to help myself, I lowered my head a fraction until my mouth was by his ear and said, "So you're a hair puller, huh?" Levi's head whipped in my direction, and when his eyes flew to my hair, I chuckled. "Good to know. I'll be sure to always leave you a few inches."

TWO

Levi

KILLIAN MICHAELS IS going to be the death of me. That was my only thought as the sexy rocker walked through the curtains to the passenger section of the plane and left me standing at the open door in danger of passing out and falling down the damn stairs.

It wasn't often that I met someone who had the ability to constantly throw me off my game. But ever since our first meeting, I'd had a difficult time drawing a professional line and staying on the right side of it. The right side of it not being *me* straddling Killian's lap, which would be my preferred seat for the trip.

It was such a shame, really, because the things I could, and would, do to that body if he was any other person on the planet made it close to impossible to be near him and not have some kind of physical reaction. But he wasn't any other person, was he? He was the bassist from the most successful rock band in the world. The same rock band I managed and looked after, and whose contract, unfortunately, did not include the words *keep said bassist satisfied in bed in any way he demands.*

"Everyone on board?" Susie, the flight attendant, asked.

I nodded. "Mind if I grab a drink before we take off?

"I can get it for you—"

"No need," I said, moving past her to grab a glass as she began to get the cabin ready for departure. I didn't need Killian to see he'd driven me to drink, so after I poured a finger of scotch, I downed it right by the closed cockpit door.

"Want me to bring you another?" she asked, but I shook my head and made my way through the curtains into the cabin. Slade and Jagger took up opposing seats to the left, already deep into a card game, while Halo and Viper had snagged their spots in the back.

That left Killian, who glanced up at me, raised an eyebrow, and then resumed staring out the window.

Spot in the front it is. I settled into the cushy seat and buckled in before raising the window shade. It definitely wasn't the smoggy view of Los Angeles that had Killian so captivated, but rather a way to ignore me, I imagined. We'd been playing that game now for months. Six months, to be exact.

I closed my eyes, thinking back to that night on the rooftop in Atlanta. Killian had pulled me away from the party, and my first thought had been that one of his bandmates was in trouble —specifically Viper, who couldn't keep his damn mouth shut if you paid him.

But when Killian had put his hand on my thigh, his intention clear, all other thoughts had fled my mind. Then he'd made his move—he kissed me. I couldn't tell you about any of the hundreds of kisses I'd had in my lifetime, but I could still remember every second of the handful of minutes I'd spent with him in the cabana. A war raged inside me then and now, half of me wanting so desperately the man I'd lusted after the moment I first laid eyes on him, and the other half clinging to the professionalism I'd instilled in myself from an early age.

I couldn't kiss Killian and not expect repercussions. I'd been in this business for over a decade, and I knew exactly what happened behind the scenes in the music world. Nothing lasted forever, not with all the temptation and greed that surrounded bands riding the high of fame. I wasn't one to think with my dick, and so even though I'd initially kissed Killian back, I'd been able to pull away. To put a stop to something that couldn't start, especially not after a night of tequila shots.

My refusal didn't come without punishment, though, namely the sharp edge of Killian's tongue. It was strange...if he wasn't lashing out at me, he was trying to tempt me into submission. Seemingly gone was the laid-back personality of the unofficial band leader, and in its place was something more...defensive.

I didn't like it, but I also knew there was nothing I could do about it unless I removed myself from the situation completely, and *that* wasn't happening. We'd both just have to get over it. Mind over matter.

"You're a fucking cheater," Slade shouted, throwing his cards down on the table that separated him and Jagger.

"Because I won? Go cry about it." Jagger scooped up the cards and shuffled them. Once he began to deal, Slade shook his head.

"No way. I'm out."

"Jealous? Should I teach you my ways?"

Slade raised his tattooed hands and lifted his middle fingers. "Tell your ways they can suck it."

As Jagger chuckled, Slade leaned out of his chair into the aisle. "Yo, Halo. Where's Imogen?"

"Why? Need someone to fix that skunk on your head?" Halo smirked, and I had to bite back a laugh. It wasn't enough for Slade to be completely covered in tattoos; he had to color the two-inch-thick strip of hair he hawked out every week. Right now it was streaked black and white, and yeah, it looked like a skunk.

"Not cool, man," Slade said, rubbing his hair.

"She usually flies with us, and she knows how to play a decent hand of Texas hold'em, unlike this fuckhead." Jagger smirked at Slade and then winced in pain when Slade kicked him in the shin.

"Im's helping out while my dad recovers from his knee surgery. She'll fly over in a few days," Halo said.

Out of the corner of my eye I saw Slade and Jagger give each other a look, and something about it made me grateful Halo was sitting in the back so he couldn't see it.

I groaned and turned back toward the window. Every one of these guys liked to play with fire, and it was only a matter of time before someone got burned.

Wouldn't be me. I had rules. I stuck to rules. I didn't break them under any circumstances—and especially not for Killian Michaels.

THREE

Killian

"IF YOU'RE JUST joining us, we've got Fallen Angel here live with us in the studio talking about their Australian tour, which kicks off this weekend here in Melbourne. Thanks for being here, guys."

"No worries," I said, grinning at the radio host across from us. "That's what you say here, right?"

"That's right, but this isn't the first time you guys have been here, is it? Well, except for your new frontman over there, Halo. How are you liking Australia so far? The natives treating you well?"

As we all looked in the angel's direction, he flashed that now-famous smile toward our host.

"I love it here, are you kidding me? There's sun, surf, and sand. Your food is off the chain, and what are those cookies I can't stop eating?" Halo looked to Viper, who grinned.

"Tim Tams?"

Halo snapped his fingers and nodded. "Yeah, those."

The host chuckled. "Ah, what's a first visit to Australia without stuffing yourself with Tim Tams? We pride ourselves on those. If us locals can't win you over, the Tim Tam will. What about Vegemite? They dare you to eat that yet?"

"*Dare* me?" Halo grimaced. "Uh, you mean it doesn't taste like Nutella?" He spun in his seat to pin Viper with an accusatory look.

"What?" Viper put his hands up. "That's what I was told."

"Mhmm." Halo shook his head. "I think you're full of it."

As much as I liked watching Viper get his balls handed to him by the angel, I said, "He really was told that. He took a whiff of it the first time we visited and refused to touch the stuff. Slade was our taste tester."

Slade lounged back in his seat, a smug look on his face. "That's right. I took one for the team. I'm always willing to try something new."

"Always?" the host said, and I almost groaned. There was no telling what would come out of Slade's mouth with that opening.

"Let's just say I've had much worse things in my mouth than Vegemite, that's for damn sure. But that's a whole other kinda interview."

When Slade added a wink, Levi, who was seated off to the side of the booth, rubbed his fingers across his forehead. Then he looked at me, his dark eyes relaying a silent but very clear message: *Bring the focus back to the band and the tour, please.*

"We love Melbourne, though," I said, and offered up my most charming grin. "The Marvel Stadium is one of our favorite venues. The crew has been working around the clock to set everything up for the back-to-back concerts coming up this weekend, and we couldn't be more pumped."

"Not sure if you've seen this, but there are already fans camped out in front of the stadium." The host held up an iPad with a video of the long line of fans decked out in Fallen Angel apparel, holding up signs as they screamed in excitement at the camera.

As we read over the messages on the signs, Viper snorted. "Looks like Jagger's got a couple of marriage proposals. Could get ugly."

"Ladies, there's plenty of me to go around," Jagger said, grinning as the rest of us groaned.

"Please stop feeding his ego. He can barely fit his head on the plane as it is." Halo elbowed Viper in the ribs, and he winced. "What?"

"Anyway," I said, trying to corral the wild circus. "I think it's awesome that the fans are hanging out, but they look a little hungry. We should probably send them some pizza." I glanced at Levi with a raised brow, and he nodded, tapping on his phone already.

"I know you've got a packed schedule while you're here, but before you go, I have to ask, will we get to see that spectacular winged piano during the show? We've all seen the pictures, and it looks like it'd be a massive undertaking to bring it all this way."

"What's an angel without his wings?" Viper said, winking at Halo before settling back in the chair beside him and throwing an arm over the back.

"So that's a yes?" the host asked.

"That's a hell yes," I said. "We've got a few surprises up our sleeves, though, trying to make each leg of the tour a bit different."

"Any hint on what those surprises might be?"

"Guess you'll have to come see the show to find out," Halo said.

"Well, I've got my tickets, but it looks like you guys are also offering up a couple of VIP tickets for two of our listeners. Can you tell us what that entails?"

"A chance to pop the question to Jagger," Slade joked.

I rolled my eyes. "What he means is a meet-and-greet before the show as well as pit tickets. You'll get a chance to hang out on stage, take a picture with the wings, grab a drink with us—"

"Hang on, can I enter this too? Because that's one hell of an amazing package," the host said.

"Come on," I said, catching Levi's eye again. This time he only smirked before focusing back on his phone, but I knew he was already taking care of anything that we threw at him. It was just the way he worked.

Smart. Efficient. Sexy. Not that the last one matters...

I forced myself to tear my eyes away, focusing back on the giveaway happening, making sure to keep the other guys on track as they cracked jokes. It seemed to always fall to me to be the one keeping shit in line, not that I minded much. It wasn't like I was the rebel bad boy—Viper—or the one always putting his foot in his mouth—Slade. I was more even-keeled, not the one to rock the boat, but to drive it. That was the only reason Levi even communicated with me at this point—because I was the one to get shit done, and he knew it.

"Guys, great interview. Thanks for being here," the host said once we wrapped things up and handed back our headphones. We all shook hands, said our goodbyes, and then headed out to the studio's back entrance.

"Hey, Killian, wait up a sec."

At Levi's familiar timbre, I paused, looking over my shoulder at where he jogged to catch up with me. The turquoise pressed pants and white button-up shouldn't have looked as good as they did on him, and I swept my eyes up and down his body before I could stop myself.

If he noticed me checking him out, he ignored it.

As the rest of the group headed out the back door to the waiting SUV, I shoved my hands in my jeans pocket and waited for Levi, determined to play it cool, determined not to touch him.

FOUR

Levi

AS THE DOOR to the back entrance closed behind Halo, leaving me standing in the empty hallway with Killian, I suddenly realized that asking him to wait behind for me probably wasn't the smartest thing I could've done—especially with how sexy he looked today.

I mean, wow, I didn't think I'd ever met a person who could make a pair of jeans and a black t-shirt look so damn hot. But with the way *U2* was stretched tight across his built chest and the sleeves hugged his biceps, it was all I could do to keep my eyes on his face.

It also didn't help that he had just checked me out. He likely hadn't even realized he was doing it, but when those blue eyes swept down over me, my cock sure as hell realized it—damn him for being so goddamn tempting.

Knowing it was too late to spit out something as mundane as *never mind*, I braced myself for my first one-on-one with him since we'd taken off from Los Angeles, determined to keep a cool head.

"What's up, Levi?" Killian's brow was creased, his tone less than cordial as I came to a stop opposite him. "Somethin' the matter?"

Other than the fact you're scowling at me when we used to have such an easy relationship? Nothing. Nothing at all.

I cleared my throat as I tightened my grip around my phone. "No, um, everything is great."

Um? What the hell is the matter with me? My mother used to tell me that *um* was for people with nothing better to say, and that was certainly not the case with me—except when I was standing only inches from Killian Michaels, apparently.

"Okaaay, then." Killian went to turn and walk away from me, but before he got one foot in front of the other, I reached out and grabbed his arm.

I hadn't meant to do it, didn't even know I was going to, but when Killian stopped and looked down at where my fingers were touching him, I became hyperaware of just how warm his bare skin was.

Hmm, I wonder if he's that hot all over—

"Levi?"

My name falling off Killian's tongue made my brain momentarily shut down to anything other than the feel of his skin, his cologne swirling around me, and the fact that I was touching him. But when he turned around to face me, I realized just how close we were standing. I drew my hand back and took a step away, knowing if I didn't find my professionalism sometime soon, this was about to escalate—and fast.

The expression in Killian's eyes now was stormy, and I couldn't tell if it was irritation or something altogether different as he took a step toward me, again closing the distance I had purposely put between us, but this time I held my ground.

"Right," I said, looking him directly in the eye. "I just wanted to say thank you for back there."

"Thank you? What for?"

"Keeping things on track." When Killian snorted, I said, "I

mean it. You always keep the guys on topic, focused. So thank you."

Killian narrowed his eyes and then took another step closer. He was so close that I actually *had* to back up or he would run into me, and as he kept coming, I realized that was exactly his intention.

"Killian," I said, but it wasn't much of a protest even to my own ears.

For the first time since I'd asked him to wait for me, Killian drew his hands out of his pockets and placed them on the wall by either side of my head. I swallowed, my admonishment getting stuck somewhere at the back of my throat as Killian lowered his eyes to my mouth and then licked his lips.

Fuck me. This was not good.

"You know..." Killian's warm breath drifted over my lips, and no one was more shocked than me when I sighed. "Since I was such a good boy today and kept everyone in the room focused, what do you think I should get for that?"

I locked my eyes on his. "You need incentive now?"

Killian's eyes darkened to a dangerous blue. "Couldn't hurt. I mean, if you want me to keep babysitting, don't you think I deserve some compensation for that?"

I scoffed. "If you think for a second I'm going to trade sex for—"

"I didn't say that," Killian said, and pushed off the wall, his lip curling. "But it's nice to see where your head went."

Heat rushed to my face. "I'm not stupid, Killian. You're not exactly asking for monetary compensation."

"Maybe I wanted you to do my fucking laundry."

"I don't even do my own laundry, so I guess you're in for disappointment."

Killian smirked. "Come on, Levi. When are you gonna admit what's going on here?"

"*Nothing* is going on here."

"Really?"

"Really."

"So if I kissed you right now"—Killian leaned forward, his breath on my cheek—"you wouldn't kiss me back?"

I pushed against his chest, but he was unmoving. "No. I wouldn't."

A low chuckle rumbled out of him, and then he whispered by my ear, "Liar."

FIVE

Killian

"ON THE COUNT of three, everyone grab a couple of pizza boxes and run out." Levi crouched by the door, ready to bust it wide as the Escalade slowed to a stop in front of the long line of fans waiting in front of Marvel Stadium. It looked like even more had lined up since we'd left the radio show, stopping only to scoop up a shit-ton of pizza, which Levi had ordered after my suggestion.

Slade rubbed his hands together. "They're gonna freak. Let's do this."

"Nice one," Jagger said, slapping his hand on my shoulder as we all waited for Levi's count.

"One, two..." Levi opened the door and jumped out. "Three."

One by one we each grabbed a few boxes, and as soon as the crowd spotted Halo emerging first, the screaming began. We had a couple of security guys with us, but since the fans were already behind a barricade, we weren't overly worried about our drop-by.

With my hands full, I stepped out of the SUV, where Levi stood, holding the door open. When we were eye to eye, I inclined my head toward the crowd. "So if I get a proposal, should I say yes?"

"You could, but that'd be hell for me."

"Oh yeah? You finally admitting you feel something for me, Levi?"

"I'm just sayin' it'd be hell to spin." He slapped me on the back, pushing me forward. "Go use some of that charm on them."

Ugh. Smug fucker.

The rest of the guys were all spread down the line, passing out pizza and stopping for selfies by the time I got to the crowd.

"Surprise," I said, handing one of the boxes over the barricade. "Thought you lovely ladies might be hungry."

"Oh my God!"

"Killian, we love you!"

"Can I have a hug? Pleeeease?"

"Look this way, Killian!"

Hands grasped at my shirt, my attention being pulled in a dozen different ways, and once I handed off all the pizza, I started down the line, grabbing their phones for selfies and saying hi to their friends on FaceTime. The sheer amount of enthusiasm aimed our way was incredible, something I no longer took for granted. After all, it wasn't that long ago that we'd been booed off stage, hitting rock bottom and forced to come up with a way to keep making music. That Fallen Angel had risen from the ashes of TBD still shocked the hell out of me, and every night we got to perform on tour had me almost falling to my knees in gratitude.

Shit, the least we could do is give them pizza and an hour of our time.

As I moved down the line, one of the girls looked familiar, and when I saw the sign lying behind her, I chuckled. "What's your name?"

"Bronwyn," she said, blushing fiercely.

"Yo, Jagger," I called out, and when he looked my way, I nodded toward her. "Bronwyn here has something she wants to ask you."

"Oh yeah?" He held up a finger to the fans he was talking to and jogged down to where Bronwyn's face had turned full-on tomato red. Ever the charmer, Jagger took her hand and kissed it. "You have a question for me, Bronwyn?"

She stuttered under the full attention Jagger aimed her way as one of her friends grabbed the sign and shoved it in her free hand. Jagger took one look at it, and then his pearly whites were on full display.

"M-m-marry me, Jagger," Bronwyn finally managed before flinging her arms around his neck and pulling him in close. Out of the corner of my eye, I saw one of our bodyguards heading toward them, but Jagger seemed to be holding his own, so I put a hand up so the bodyguard wouldn't interfere.

Jagger leaned in to Bronwyn and whispered something in her ear, causing the girl's eyes to go swoony, and then he planted a kiss on her cheek and headed back to where he'd been before I called him over.

"So? What'd he say?" I asked.

Bronwyn shook her head and pretended to zip her lips.

"Hold on a second, I should get some damn credit for this," I said, feigning annoyance. "I mean, you two could get married because of me. You're welcome."

The girls all laughed, and I moved on down the line, and as my eyes drifted over the sea of people, they locked on to Viper, who was busy signing and smiling with fans, but was also standing close enough to Halo that I knew he was watching to make sure no one got too close—no one touched what was his.

A little closer to me were Jagger and Slade, and as I watched the two of them play off one another to the crowd, who ate it up, I realized that I was the only one standing here amongst hundreds of fans…alone.

I looked over my shoulder, and my eyes caught on Levi where he stood leaning against the SUV, his legs crossed and his eyes glued to his phone, and I knew exactly who I'd choose to be walking beside me to help hand out these pizzas— problem was that Levi was more interested in having a relationship with his phone than me, so…

Hmm, wait a second. Pulling out my phone, I took a step back from the crowd for a minute and brought up Levi's number. Then I quickly typed, **Thinking of more lies to tell me or yourself?**

A few seconds later, Levi's head shot up, and when I arched a brow, a scowl crossed his full lips, and my dick immediately stood up and took notice.

Okay, who knew *that* would get me off. But there was no denying it. As Levi spun away from me to watch over everyone else, I couldn't help smirking, knowing that I'd gotten under his skin one way or another. Seemed only fair, right?

SIX

Levi

LATER THAT NIGHT, I stood in the luxury suite of the hotel and stared out the wall of windows that overlooked the gorgeous Yarra River. The lights from the casino, restaurants, and shops twinkled off the water and made a stunning view as I checked my phone for New York's time.

It was early morning there, but not too early that I'd be waking my brother if I called now. Not that I thought Liam would mind the interruption, considering the news I was about to deliver.

As I hit Liam's number and waited for it to connect, I ran a hand through my hair and thought about the insane reaction from the crowd today. It'd been one hell of a smart idea on Killian's behalf, as much as I hated to admit it. Not only for the fans but for the press. It made the guys of Fallen Angel seem accessible, relatable.

I was struggling right now when it came to keeping my distance from Fallen Angel's bassist. It was hard enough to resist Killian when he was being a temperamental shit, but when he focused all his attention on me, it was a miracle I didn't grab him and finish what he seemed hellbent on starting every time he looked at me these days. And God did I want to finish it.

I hadn't had a date, kiss, or relationship of any kind since taking this job. Every single minute of my day from the moment I'd said yes to managing the band had been consumed with making sure the guys of Fallen Angel stayed out of trouble but stayed *in* the spotlight. Not an easy feat when you had someone like Viper to keep an eye on. But that left little time for myself, little time to go looking for some relief from the frustration I felt in such close proximity to the one I wanted but couldn't have.

So instead, I worked myself until I literally fell into bed, and that way, I stayed busy. That way, I wasn't sitting around thinking about the fact that Killian Michaels' hotel room was two doors down and he would be more than welcoming if I gave in to the lust I couldn't seem to shake.

"Hello."

I startled at Liam's voice, so caught up in imagining what Killian would be wearing if I *were* to knock on his door, that I'd completely forgotten I'd even placed a call.

"Hello?" Liam said again, and I cleared my throat and answered.

"G'day, mate. How the hell are you?" I winced at my terrible imitation of an Australian accent, but when my brother let out a booming laugh, I figured it was worth it.

"Oh my God. That was horrible." When he finally got his laughter down to a mere chuckle, he added, "Can you do it again so I can record it?"

A smile crossed my lips. "How about no, and you better start being nice to me. I'm calling you with a surprise..."

"I mean, you better be, it's early here, and I—"

"Early? It's nearly seven, so stop your complaining." I leaned against the window frame and grinned. "I *could* always call someone more grateful and give *them* this VIP ticket to

Sydney's sold-out Fallen Angel concert. Not to mention the first-class plane ticket that will be waiting at LaGuardia International to whisk them away to Melbourne, where they'll take a private jet *with* Fallen Angel..."

"Are you fucking kidding me?"

"Oh, hello? Are you suddenly awake, brother?"

There was a pause for a second, probably Liam trying to pick his jaw up off the floor. "Did you really just say what I think you said?"

"I don't know, what do you think I said?"

"That I'm going to fucking Australia to see Fallen Angel. Don't play with me, Le. You know that's what you fucking said."

I started laughing. "I mean, it's all dependent on whether or not you can get the old man to give you the time off."

"Umm, he owes me, so I'm good there. You finally going to introduce me to your new bosses?"

Liam had been bugging me for months now to meet the guys, and while I knew they wouldn't care if I'd brought him around for an introduction, I hadn't wanted to come off as taking advantage. I was trying to make a good impression. This, however, was a little different. Liam was family, and they'd given me the ticket to use, so...I thought it would be okay if I set up a little meet-and-greet for the guy. He was, after all, a huge fan.

"Yeah, yeah. You'll get to meet them. As long as you promise not to embarrass me."

"When have I ever embarrassed you?"

"There have been too many times to count. But I think you'll fit right in. At least I won't have to worry about you hitting on them."

Liam chuckled. "Mhmm. Not really my type. But don't think I won't be sizing that Killian guy up—"

"Killian? Why would you be—"

"Oh, come on, Le. You don't think I've noticed how much you talk about him?"

I pushed off the window frame, my spine stiffening. "That's because *he* happens to be a pain in my ass."

"Uh, TMI, bro."

"What? No, I didn't mean literally. Jesus. And on that note, you ungrateful little shit, I'm hanging up."

"You're hanging up because I'm right—"

I ended the call. I'd email Liam the details later.

The last thing I needed to think about as I got into bed tonight was Killian, and the fact that even Liam noticed that the sexy rocker had managed to get under my skin.

SEVEN

Levi

_____

WITH THE PRINTED schedule for the first Melbourne show in my hand, I punched the down button for the elevator and stepped inside. I'd already emailed the itinerary to each of the guys, but it made me feel better to personally hand over the play-by-play so they couldn't argue they hadn't checked their phone.

Musicians. What no one told you about the job was that you were sometimes the glorified babysitter.

The elevator door opened to one of the hotel's restaurants, where Halo had told me the guys were having brunch, and I spotted them out on the terrace. It was a warm, sunny day, and a light breeze rippled through the patio as I stepped outside.

"Morning," I said, shielding my eyes as I glanced over each of them, making sure they weren't struggling to recover from any late-night parties I didn't know about. But no one looked hungover or any worse for wear...though there was one person missing from the table. "Where's Killian?"

"Still in bed," Halo answered.

"Why?"

Viper stabbed at something on Halo's plate and brought it

to his lips. "Maybe he's got a hot reason to be there."

My stomach turned, an unexpected reaction, but I kept my expression neutral. "Is that a fact?"

"The fuck should I know?" Viper said between chews. "But that's usually the only reason he doesn't turn up for breakfast."

Right. Of course. It wasn't like I didn't know any one of these guys could have visitors at any hour, but Killian had always kept anything he did on the down-low, so even I hadn't heard about it.

"That for us?" Jagger nodded at the papers in my hand.

"Uh, yeah." Straightening, like I wasn't affected in the slightest by Killian's absence—because I wasn't—I passed the itineraries around the table. "Pickup is at one at the back entrance. Don't be late."

Turning on my heel, I swung open the door as Slade said, "Did you wanna join? No? All righty, then."

No, I wouldn't be joining. Instead, I'd punish myself by knocking on Killian's door to hand-deliver the schedule and make sure he wasn't passed out in his own puke.

And while I was there, maybe kick out any overnight guests. You know, to keep him on track for the day's activities.

Yeah, sure, that's why you're heading upstairs to his room. It's not because you want to catch him with someone so maybe this ridiculous attraction will go the hell away.

"Shut up," I said, just as the elevator door opened, an older couple staring at me peculiarly.

Great, now I'm talking to myself.

I cleared my throat and forced a smile as I stepped out. "Morning," I said, before hurrying past them down the hall. The strange twisting in my stomach felt uncomfortably like... nerves? That couldn't be right. I didn't get nervous. I wasn't an anxious person. So why, the closer I got to Killian's room, did I feel like I would pass out?

Mentally slapping myself, I took a deep breath and rapped

on his door before I could think twice about it. When there was no answer, I knocked a little harder.

Still nothing.

"Killian? Answer the door." After a few seconds, I pressed my ear against the door, preparing myself for the moans and groans I expected to hear after Viper's comment, but it was silent.

Shit. He wasn't really passed out in his own puke, right? That wasn't Killian. But why wasn't he answering the door? Maybe I needed to call downstairs and have them give me the key or—

The door swung open, and as I jerked back, I got an eyeful of exactly why Killian hadn't answered.

His dark hair was wet and slicked back from his face, and water dripped from the ends down his strong neck. In his hand, he held together the edges of a white robe, barely keeping it closed, and I could see the way his tanned skin glistened like he'd just walked out of the shower.

Good God. The entire way up here I'd been preparing to give him a dressing down over his reckless behavior. But as I stood there completely gobsmacked over just how dressed down he already *was*, all of my lectures vanished in the blink of an eye.

"Jesus, Levi, is the place on fire or something?"

The place wasn't on fire, but he certainly was. *Holy shit. Why did I think it was smart to come up here again?* If someone had asked me right then, I wouldn't have had an answer.

"Levi?"

At the sound of my name, I somehow managed to drag my greedy eyes away from the strip of naked skin I could see between the lapels of Killian's robe.

When Killian had first pulled open the door, there'd been a mix of confusion and irritation swirling in his eyes. But now his expression had turned to one I'd seen only a handful of times. It was an expression that was about to get me in a whole lot of trouble if I didn't hurry up and get the hell out of there.

"Hi," I said, and when Killian smiled, making his gorgeous face impossible to look away from, my next words left my brain.

Killian put a hand up on the doorframe, and the move made his robe gape open at his chest, something my dick was not unaware of.

"Hi..."

When I realized he was waiting for me to say something in return, I glanced down at the paper in my hand and then quickly held it up. "Your schedule," I said.

Killian lowered his eyes to the paper, but instead of taking it, he looked back up at me and said, "Did you change something on it?"

I frowned. "No. Why?"

"Well, you already sent it this morning. To my email?"

My mouth fell open as I tried to come up with some sort of response, but I was drawing a blank. But could anyone blame me? Killian was standing in front of me with what I was positive was absolutely nothing on beneath that damn robe, talking to me as though this was an everyday occurrence for us.

It was not.

"Oh for God's sake, Killian. You know the drill," I said, annoyed that I sounded flustered in the face of all of...well, him. Then, deciding I needed to take back some of my control, I took a step forward and slapped the paper against that chest I'd just been admiring. "Stop trying to distract me and take the damn schedule."

As soon as my hand came up against solid muscle, I realized my error. But it wasn't until Killian wrapped his fingers around my wrist that I knew this was a mistake I'd been wanting to make for a long time now.

"Is that what I'm doing? Distracting you?"

EIGHT

Killian

I USUALLY PRIDED myself on being able to read a person, but as Levi stood in my hallway with his hand against my chest, I couldn't tell if he wanted to kill me or climb me like a tree. It was a toss-up, really.

"*No*, you are not distracting me." Levi quickly snatched his hand back, then looked down the hall before bringing his fiery eyes back to mine. "Do you always answer your door like this?"

Liking the fact that Levi was more flustered than I could ever remember seeing him, I slowly looked down to the robe I was barely holding shut and thought, what the hell.

I let go of the lapels and placed one hand on the doorjamb, and the robe fell wide open, exposing my freshly showered skin. "Like what?"

"You're...you're..."

"Naked?"

"Yes," Levi said, and as his eyes took a quick tour of my body, I had no hope of controlling what it did next. As my cock stiffened, Levi's eyes flew back to mine. "I know you're naked."

"Well, you couldn't seem to spit it out, so..."

Levi gestured to the robe. "Would you cover yourself before someone sees you?"

"Why? Worried it'll show up in the magazines tomorrow?"

Levi's glare was so fierce that I probably should've dropped dead.

"No. But you should be. I just got everyone back to talking about the *music* this band makes." Levi fumed, his eyes dropping again to *all* that was on display. "The last thing I need to deal with is your dick splashed all over the country."

I shrugged. "I don't know, could be good publicity. You can't seem to keep your eyes off it."

Levi's gaze flew back to mine, and I grinned.

"You think you're really funny, don't you?"

"I prefer the terms charming and…huge."

Levi rolled his eyes. "You're ridiculous. Cover yourself up, *now*."

Something about his pissy tone had every rebellious instinct rising to the surface. So I let go of the door, took a step back into my hotel room, and dropped my robe to the floor at my feet.

"Whoops," I said as Levi's jaw nearly hit the floor. "There goes my robe."

Levi balled his fists by his side. "Pick that up."

"No." I lowered my eyes to the crumpled schedule in Levi's fist. "Um, don't you need to give that to me?"

"Huh?"

That non-answer was like a well-placed stroke to my…ego. "The schedule," I said, and pointed at Levi's hand again. "Aren't you gonna come in here and give it to me?"

Levi looked down at the paper and then back to me, and the annoyance radiating off him was palpable. "You want me to give it to you, do you?"

Somehow I didn't think what I wanted and what he was offering were the same things. But because I was a glutton for fucking punishment when it came to Levi Walker, I nodded and said, "Yes, I really do."

Levi balled the paper the rest of the way up and threw it at my forehead, and as I ducked out of the way, I saw him turn on his heel and stalk off, the door slamming shut in his wake.

NINE

Killian

THE DRUMS KICKED in heavy on the night of our final Melbourne show before the blue spotlights flashed on overhead, lighting me up as we played the opening notes of "Invitation," one of our biggest hits on the new album. It sent the crowd wild, their screams all I could hear even as Halo began to sing.

Sweat beaded along my brow, the air getting hotter on stage the longer we played. I'd already peeled off my jacket, leaving me in a short-sleeved shirt I was tempted to toss like Viper had done a few songs ago.

My eyes caught on one of the signs a few rows back that said, "You're so sexy you KILL me dead." I shot the sign owner a wink and then looked over as Halo sauntered my way. Our frontman had only gotten more confident over the course of touring, and I could see the change in him even from the domestic leg we'd finished a couple months ago. I'd known from the moment I laid eyes on Halo's audition tape that he'd be the right man to take over the spot our ex-singer had left, even if I'd been met with resistance at first. Namely from Viper, who really should be thanking me every damn day of his life.

Halo leaned against me, his back to mine, his voice as strong and deep as ever as I plucked at the strings. As I faced the wings, my gaze landed on Levi offstage, his hand on the earpiece he wore. When he caught me watching him, he crossed his arms, that defiance from earlier emerging as he stared my way.

Damn, he was hot, even scowling. Those full lips were set in a line I wanted to lick open, and as that thought crossed my mind, I bit down suggestively on my bottom lip and rocked my hips forward. Levi looked down my body before he could stop himself.

That's right. Look all you want. Just like you did yesterday when I dropped my robe.

Levi could say all day that it was his job to watch us, but I knew better.

Behind my bass guitar, my cock twitched, and I was grateful that I had an instrument to cover myself. Hell, that was probably why I'd started playing bass instead of singing in the first place: nowhere to hide behind a mic stand.

As if he knew exactly what I was thinking about, Levi met my eyes again. I licked my lips and winked before turning my attention back to the crowd, just as Halo launched into the final chorus.

The roar of the crowd was infectious, their energy infusing my body, hyping me up and throwing that energy back their way.

"Hey, Kill, why don't you come over here for a minute," Halo said, waving me over once the song was finished.

I ran a hand through my sweat-soaked hair and started his way, but I almost stopped when I looked past where Halo stood and saw the gleam in Viper's eyes.

Oh God, what now?

"So, we need to let you all in on a little secret," Halo said, grabbing my shoulder and giving it a squeeze. "This guy right here, maybe you know him? Some might say he's a sexy bastard—"

There was a loud reaction, and someone in the front row yelled, "We love you, Killian!"

"He loves you too," Halo said, grinning. "As a matter of fact, he loves you so much he wanted to play for you on his birthday."

Oh Jesus, no way.

I started to turn away, but Viper grabbed my arm and forced me back toward the audience.

"Where ya goin, my man?"

I looked between Viper and Halo and shook my head. "Fuck you both."

"Such a mouth on this guy," Viper said. "You know, we looked all over for a special birthday hat for Kill to wear while we sing to him, and it wasn't easy, but…"

"We figured since we're here in Australia and there are no sombreros, an Akubra would have to do," Jagger said, walking up from behind and placing something on my head.

"What the fuck is in my face?" I said, reaching up to remove the hat, or whatever an Akubra was, but Viper and Jagger weren't having that. Strings hung down in front of my face every few inches with what looked like a cork on the end of each one.

Was it mandated somewhere that you had to look ridiculous on your birthday? In front of a crowd of tens of thousands?

I glared at Jagger. "I expected better from you."

"Why? I think you look very striking. I can hardly see your face." When Jagger gave me a brilliant white smile, I responded with a finger.

The fans were obviously enjoying my pain, laughter ringing out through the stadium, as well as whoops and cheers. I suspected they approved of the guys' choice of apparel, which, as Halo soon explained, was an Australian hat usually worn in the bush to keep the flies out of your face.

Pity it didn't work on humans.

As Slade joined the rest of us at the front of the stage, he said, "On the count of three, we want you to sing 'Happy Birthday' as loud as you can to this motherfucker."

Viper shoved me forward, singling me out center stage as the rest of the guys spread out, counted down, and then began to lead the crowd in the loudest rendition of "Happy Birthday" I'd ever heard in my life.

I looked out—past the hanging corks—at the people singing along all over the sold-out stadium, and couldn't help but smile. Many of the fans had their cell phones lifted high, the flashlights turned on so it looked like the stadium was full of stars. About halfway through the song, I felt someone come up beside me, and when I turned, I realized it was Levi…holding a birthday cake covered in candles.

The flames illuminated his gorgeous eyes that, for once, weren't glaring my way. As the song came to a close, Levi lifted the cake up slightly, and it didn't take me long to think of my wish.

With my eyes on Levi, I smirked and then blew out the candles as the audience cheered.

"So? Did you make a wish?" Levi said, his voice barely audible over the crowd.

"I did. Feel like making it come true?"

That glower I was getting so familiar with returned. Grinning, I swiped some icing off the side of the cake and sucked it off my pointer finger suggestively, causing Levi to turn on his heel and march offstage before I even swallowed.

So much for having my cake and eating it too.

As Slade and Jagger took up their positions at their instruments, I tore off the hat and flung it like a Frisbee out into the crowd.

"Happy birthday, man," Viper said, slapping me on the back, and then he leaned in to whisper, "Hope your liver's ready for the afterparty."

I groaned, already imagining the epic hangover I'd have come morning. But they were usually worth it, and since tonight would be all about me, maybe my wish would come true after all.

As long as I didn't have to wear that damn cork hat.

TEN

Levi

THE PARTY WAS in full swing by the time I made my way to the casino across the street from our hotel, where Killian's birthday party was taking place in one of the clubs. I'd purposely waited until things were well underway, busying myself with making sure everything was wrapped up here for the Melbourne portion of the tour before we headed to Sydney tomorrow. It would be much easier to make an appearance at the party if Killian's attention was already divided between a packed room of guests, and that was exactly what I faced when I entered the private club through velvet curtains.

"Where the fuck have you been?"

Before my eyes could even adjust to the dizzying array of colored lights flashing through the dark room, Viper was by my side, thrusting a shot into my hand.

I hadn't planned on drinking anything tonight, but now that I was here, maybe it wasn't a bad idea to relieve some of the stress. I threw the shot back, and Viper raised his brow.

"Gonna be one of those nights, huh?" With a gleam in his eye, he handed me another shot, which I swallowed down, the whiskey making my eyes water. When he turned around to grab yet another off the bar, Halo cut him off.

"If you're not planning on holding his hair tonight, you need to slow your roll," Halo said.

Viper licked his lips as he wrapped his finger around one of Halo's curls. "You know I've got better plans tonight."

"Then stop trying to get Levi shitfaced. Such a bad influence." Halo grinned my way as Viper moved in close behind him, his mouth on Halo's neck. When he whispered something I couldn't hear into Halo's ear and a flush creeped into his cheeks, I'd had enough.

Rolling my eyes, I reached for the shot Viper had left on the bar and threw it back before he could protest, and then made my way through the thick of the crowd.

The alcohol making its way through my veins was making me hot already, and I loosened the knot at my throat and unbuttoned the collar. It meant I wouldn't look dressed to impress, but who was I here to impress, anyway?

Not Killian, that's for sure.

Speaking of the birthday boy, he was holding court on the far side of the room by the floor-to-ceiling windows, surrounded on all sides by admirers, laughing and drinking. I wasn't surprised in the least. Killian had an infectious smile that lit up the room and a charm that made others want to be around him. Hell, he'd been the one to convince me to take this job, though if I'd known how difficult that would be, maybe I would've thought twice about it.

Being attracted to Killian was easy; it was the staying-away part that was difficult.

Which brought me back to the reason I'd ventured this way in the first place: to look for a one-night distraction.

I grabbed a shooter from one of the waitresses working the floor and instantly regretted downing whatever that fruity purple concoction was. Shuddering as my head began to swim,

I loosened my tie even more, and then a deep voice was in my ear.

"Care to dance?"

I whirled around, moving a little too fast for the amount of alcohol I'd taken in a handful of minutes, but luckily the man who'd propositioned me was there, his hand on my hip to steady me.

The man was several inches taller than me and built like a linebacker. He was handsome, with dark, smooth skin and bright eyes that weren't swimming with alcohol the way mine were.

"Hi," I managed, fully aware of his hand on my hip—as well as a pair of eyes boring holes into the side of my head. I glanced to my left, my eyes instantly meeting Killian's from across the room. I inclined my head.

You don't like this, huh? Too fucking bad.

I turned back to the man on the dance floor and smiled. "I'd love to dance with you."

"Good," he said, curling his fingers around my belt loops and pulling me forward so that our bodies were flush with one another. Damn, he was nothing but solid muscle, like grinding on a boulder, and I had to grab his arms to stay as close as I wanted to.

Closing my eyes, I tried to relax and let my body go along with what I'd come here to do, but my mind was swirling with images of Killian. Killian glaring at me, Killian blowing out the candles on his cake as we sang "Happy Birthday" in front of a crowd of tens of thousands, and, of course, Killian dropping his robe so his perfect, naked body was on full display and could be imprinted in my brain forever—ensuring that in moments like this, when I wanted to think of anything but him, it'd pop up to torture me.

What was that saying? Always wanting what you can't have? That didn't usually apply to me, but ever since meeting

Killian, it'd been a struggle to think of much else. I could deal with my attraction so much better if I hadn't known he felt the same way.

Why couldn't he just keep his damn mouth shut? Why did he have to complicate everything and kiss me that night? Why did I have to kiss him back? Because now that I knew what I was missing, it was hard for anyone else to compare.

I opened my eyes, the images of Killian fading as I focused my attention back on my dance partner. His hips moved in time to the beat as I matched his pace, but even though he was an attractive, and seriously built, guy, something just didn't feel quite right. But I could still feel Killian's stare, so I ignored it and kept on dancing.

And maybe I'd have another one of those disgusting fruity shots when the waitress came back around.

ELEVEN

Killian

"IS THAT LEVI out there?" Slade came up beside me where I stood by the wall of windows trying to understand what exactly I was seeing, and as I tried to wrap my brain around it, I came up with absolutely...nothing.

"Oh my God, it is." Slade chuckled and elbowed me in the side. "You getting a look at this or what?"

Oh, I was getting a look at it, all right. I'd been getting a front-row view of Levi Walker getting hit on by some brick wall of a guy, ever since he'd walked out onto the dance floor looking sexy as hell and totally off-limits.

I'd been waiting for Levi to arrive for what seemed like hours. I had no idea how long it'd actually been with the copious amounts of alcohol everyone had kept sending my way. But the second our illustrious manager had set foot inside the club, my Levi radar had gone off and I hadn't been able to tear my eyes away from him since.

He knew it, too.

Levi had thrown back more alcohol in the last thirty minutes than I'd seen him drink in all the time I'd known him. And as though he were out to prove a point tonight, namely that the attraction he was feeling for me—and he was definitely feeling it—didn't exist, he'd latched on to the first tree trunk who asked him to dance.

"Dude," Slade said, trying to get my attention, but there was no way I was taking my eyes off what was happening on that dance floor. "Is he plastered? I mean, he looks kinda wobbly on his feet, no?"

I stepped away from the crowd to take a closer look, and Viper and Halo sidled up beside me.

"What are we lookin' at?" Viper said, as he slung his arm around Halo's shoulders.

Slade gestured to the dance floor and, helpful as ever, filled my pain-in-the-ass best friend in. "Levi. Bumpin' and grindin' on some dude out there."

"You don't say?"

"Yeah, man," Slade continued. "I don't know what got into him tonight, but looks like our manager is getting his freak on."

Slade's words made my gut tighten. I didn't want to imagine Levi getting his freak on with anyone but me. But at the same time, I didn't want the guys talking about him behind his back—not that he could see us with that behemoth standing between him and us.

I glared at Slade. "You're a gossipy little shit, anyone ever tell you that? He's just dancing; there's no harm in that."

"I don't know about that," Viper said. "His hands on that guy's ass makes me thinketh he wants a lot more than a dance tonight."

"Viper…" Halo said, but that just made Viper chuckle.

"What? I mean, it's obvious he's looking for a good time. And it's not like a *better* option has shown up."

I whipped my head to the side to pin Viper with my best death stare.

"When are you gonna get over the fact he said no? Get the

fuck over it and go and try again. It's not like you to give up so easy."

"Viper," I growled. Jesus, he had a big fucking mouth.

"Wait…" Slade said. "You and Levi?"

"No," I said between clenched teeth, because honestly, the fact that the answer was a no was becoming more and more frustrating with every damn word these idiots were uttering.

"He made a move and Levi rejected him," Halo said, and I wasn't at all surprised that he knew the details, considering Viper couldn't keep his mouth shut to save his fucking self.

"Oh, *burn*, bro." Slade nodded and looked back out to the dance floor. "But it *is* your birthday…"

"Yeah," Viper added, and shoved me in the shoulder, urging me toward the floor. "So stop standing over here like a pussy and go and get what you fucking want."

I looked back to where couples of all persuasions were busy getting down and dirty to an extra-filthy song, and thought fuck it. Viper was right. It was my goddamn birthday, and if I wanted to dance with Levi, then I was going to go over there and dance with him.

As I weaved through the hot, sweaty bodies moving in time to the throbbing beat, I kept my eyes on the target and saw him grab mountain man's ass a little tighter.

So Levi wants to grind on someone tonight, does he? I could work with that. I decided a sneak attack would be my best bet and made my way around the two I couldn't tear my eyes off.

I circled them like a shark might its prey, and as I came up behind Levi, I clenched my fists by my sides. The tree had his big paws all over Levi's tight, lithe body, and I was done.

"'Scuse me?" I tapped Levi's shoulder for extra emphasis just in case he wanted to pretend not to hear me. But when he glanced over his shoulder and saw me standing there, I was more than a little happy to note those usually irritated eyes were wide with shock.

"Killian?"

"Yeah, hi," I said, and then looked to the one still holding on to *my* birthday present—well, the one I was about to give myself. "Mind if I cut in?"

Levi's mouth fell open, but before he could say anything, the mountain was dumb enough to say, "Actually—"

"Good," I said, and snatched Levi's arm. "I didn't think you would." And before either man could protest or realize what I was doing, I hauled Levi into my arms. It wasn't like the mountain would challenge me—I had security here, after all, and it *was* my birthday.

Levi stumbled into my arms and brought his hands up to steady himself. He pressed his palms to my chest, and as the warmth of them penetrated my shirt I hummed in the back of my throat.

"That was rude," Levi said, but when I wound an arm around his waist and brought him flush against my body, he seemed to lose his words.

"Ask me if I care." Levi swallowed, and when he went to move his hands away, I lowered my mouth to his ear and said, "Don't push me away. Not tonight." Then I raised my head and grinned. "It's my birthday."

Levi's lips twitched. "You think you're really charming, don't you?"

I slid my hand down to Levi's ass, and when he sucked in a breath, I said, "I *am* charming. Otherwise you would've told me to go to hell and gone back to Mr. Muscle."

Levi arched a brow, and as his lower body bumped up against my thigh, I felt his erection graze mine.

"That for me or him?" I said before I could stop myself, and as Levi opened his mouth to answer, I shook my head. "No. I don't want to know. But Levi?"

Levi licked his full, plump lips. "Yeah?"

"By the time I'm done with you out here tonight, it's gonna be *all* for me."

I brought my other hand down to his tight ass, and when I pulled him in so that his hard cock was pressed fully up against mine, I rocked forward and let him know the effect he had on me.

"Feel that?" I said in a low whisper just for him.

Levi's usually sharp, clear eyes focused on my face. They were dark, dilated, and slightly glazed as his fingers curled in my shirt.

"Just so there's no mistake"—I thrust my hips forward, grinding my stiff dick up against his—"*that* is all for you."

"Killian…" Levi said, his voice a breathy sigh that ghosted over my lips, and if there weren't hundreds of people with cell phones waiting for the next photo op, I would've said to hell with it and kissed that slick, swollen mouth. But a dance in a crowded club was one thing, a kiss—especially the kind I wanted to give him—was a whole other thing, a "front page of a gossip magazine" thing, and I wouldn't do that to Levi.

"Hmm," I said as he smoothed his hands down my torso. "I don't think my name has ever sounded so fucking good in all my life." I put my lips to his temple and said, "Say it again."

"Fuck."

I chuckled. "Well, that's not what I asked for, but…"

Levi shook his head and then lowered it, and what do you know, it fit perfectly under my chin.

"Killian, we can't do this. You—"

I rolled my hips forward, and a soft groan left Levi. "I…?"

Levi slipped his warm fingers under the hem of my shirt, and a growl left my throat.

"Christ, Levi."

When he brought his eyes up to meet mine, the raw lust staring back at me made my dick ache. I touched my fingers to his jaw, and as I trailed them down to his chin and took hold of it, I had a feeling if I kissed him, Levi wouldn't put up much protest —if any. But the song was coming to an end, and so was my patience. I'd gotten what I wanted for my birthday—my hands on him, his hands on me—and for tonight, that would have to do.

With his hips moving against mine in a throbbing rhythm, I lowered my hand to his tie, wound it around my hand, and tugged him forward until my lips were hovering an inch above his. "Now I *know* that's all for me."

Levi blinked, those gorgeous eyes roving all over my face. "It's always for you. Always…"

Holy shit. Did he just—

"Shots for the birthday boy!" As the shout penetrated my lust-addled mind, Levi's eyes darted over my shoulder, and he took in a deep breath before slowly extricating himself from my arms.

I reluctantly let him go, and as we were surrounded by friends and the rest of my bandmates, who were each holding a shot or two out to us, I looked at Levi and wondered just how much of this he would remember the next day.

TWELVE

Killian

SOMEHOW, I WOKE up the morning after my epic birthday party without a hangover, but as the rest of the guys stumbled into my suite around noon, I realized that couldn't be said for anyone else.

"Need some coffee?" My lips quirked as each of them collapsed into a chair, couch, or, as Slade seemed to prefer, the floor. "I've got a pot ready—"

"Just one?" Jagger said, not even bothering to open his eyes. Even feeling like shit, he wore an immaculate fitted suit and diamond studs in his ears, putting all of us to shame.

"Hey, asshole, this isn't room service," I said, pouring some of the hot brew into mugs. From the look of things, if I didn't want to powwow with a half-dead band, I'd need to start another pot, stat. I passed steaming mugs to each of the guys and then tossed a bunch of creamer, sugar packets, and straws on the coffee table.

Slade lifted his head off the floor, one eye barely opening. "How the hell are you functioning? I saw you do all those shots."

I shrugged. "Maybe I know how to handle my liquor."

"Bullshit," Viper said with a groan. "It was all those fruity purple bastards Halo made us shoot."

Halo's mouth fell open. "Don't put this on me. I didn't force those shots down your throat."

Viper cocked his head toward his boyfriend. "No, you forced something else down my throat…"

As Halo flushed, I poured the rest of the coffee into my mug and then rinsed the pot out so I could get another round started. If the guys were feeling this bad, I couldn't imagine the state of Levi once he arrived.

As a matter of fact… I glanced at the clock, frowning. Levi was never late, but he'd been unsteady on his feet not long after arriving at the party last night, so maybe I needed to go check on him. Hell, a drunk Levi was the only reason I hadn't pushed things further; I hadn't wanted to take advantage and wanted him to have a clear head so there would be no regrets.

Once I added some fresh grounds to the machine and hit start, I shoved my key card in my pocket so I could go check on Levi—I knew none of these fuckers would get up to let us back in—but a knock on the door sounded before I could leave.

I opened the door to see Levi standing there, not a trace of a hangover on his handsome face, though he didn't look quite like himself somehow. Maybe it was the plain navy shirt and dark jeans that were throwing me off, or maybe it was the hat he wore, or hell, maybe both. A casual Levi was a shock to the system, but hey, maybe it was laundry day. He was still fucking gorgeous. I wondered if he remembered what he'd said to me last night.

It's always for you. Always…

"Killian…hi." A nervous smile crossed Levi's lips.

Nervous? Yeah, he definitely remembered, but I didn't see any regret in his eyes, which I took as a positive sign.

Leaning against the doorjamb, I ran my eyes up and down his body before letting my gaze linger at his hips. "I was just coming to see if you needed any help getting...up." I reached out, curling my finger around one of his belt loops, and tugged him forward. "So...is this still all for me?"

"Uh..."

"No need to be shy." As I leaned in to graze my lips against his jaw, I felt his body go rigid, and then an all-too-familiar voice down the hall said, "What the fuck are you doing to my brother?"

Huh?

I jerked my head to the left, where Levi stood with sunglasses on and his mouth open in disbelief, and then looked back to the man I had a hold of.

What the fuck? Now I'm seeing two of him? Maybe I'm still drunk after all...

"Killian," the Levi to my left said, as he started down the hall, his jaw clenched. "Let Liam go."

Liam? Who the hell is Liam? Dropping my hands like I'd been burned, I stared at the man in front of me. His eyes were wide, and he swallowed hard, tightly grasping the papers in his hands.

"What the hell is going on?" I said.

Levi stepped up beside me and shoved his glasses up onto his head. "As far as I can tell, you were about to make out with my brother. You make it a habit to kiss every person who knocks on your hotel door?"

Caught off guard, I tried to make sense of the information Levi was firing my way, and as pieces of it began to fit together, I tore my eyes from his fuming face and looked back to Liam looking completely and utterly bewildered.

"I...I'm..." I started to make some lame attempt of an apology, but as the words got stuck on my tongue and the word *brother* began a loop in my head, I spun back to Levi. "This is your brother?"

Levi narrowed his eyes on me like I was a fucking moron, and he wasn't far off, because of course the guy was Levi's brother—he was the spitting image of him.

"How was I supposed to know the brother that was coming to visit you was your *twin* brother?" I ran a hand through my hair, totally thrown off my game as I stared into the exact same face as the man still standing outside my door. This face however, was scowling, and much more Levi than the nervous version I'd been about to kiss a couple of seconds ago.

"You weren't." Levi eyed me as though he was equal parts disgusted and disappointed. "But of all the guys, I figured *you* would be the one to tell us apart. Now, are you going to move or continue the amazing first impression you're making here?"

Firmly put in my place, I stepped aside, shame heating my face as Levi looked to his brother and gestured him to come inside. As he went to walk by, Liam glanced at me from under his hat and offered up a half-smile.

"Sorry for the confusion. It's really, uh…nice to meet you. I'm a huge fan."

If I could've crawled under a rock, I would've. Instead, with Levi all but glaring a hole through me over his brother's shoulder, I plastered on my most winning smile and waved it off.

"Nah, it's all good. Nothing to be sorry for. If anything, I should be apologizing." I looked to Levi and added, "It was an *innocent* mistake."

Liam nodded. "It happens all the time with people who don't know us."

Levi's spine stiffened, and I knew exactly what he was thinking. *I should've known. If I was as into him as I said I was, I should've known.* But come on, I was recovering from a late night, ten million drinks, and…and…yeah, Levi's expression as he turned to follow his brother inside the suite told me that those excuses were not gonna cut it.

Just when I thought we'd moved forward two steps, I'd taken three massive ones back. At this rate I'd be lucky if Levi looked my way the rest of the day, let alone gave me a chance to get him alone to apologize.

THIRTEEN

Levi

———

MY HEAD HAD been killing me ever since I woke this morning, but courtesy of that little shitshow in the hall with Killian and Liam, it was now throbbing like a sonofabitch.

Still fuming over what I had walked in on, I barely said a word as I directed my brother into Killian's suite, where the guys were sprawled out like a Mack truck had just run them all over. They looked...well, about as good as I felt. Slade hadn't even made it to a couch and was spread out on the floor as though his legs had collapsed from right under him, and Halo and Viper both wore sunglasses to shield their eyes—much like I had.

Killian's suite had a wall of windows overlooking the Yarra River, and right now the sun was lighting up the room as though it were inside, adding a piercing, eye-watering pain to the headaches we were already sporting.

"Um..." As we stopped just outside the circle of...dead, Liam leaned into my side and whispered, "Are you sure it's okay I'm here? I don't want to bug them when—"

"Good morning, guys," I said, much more chipper than I felt, not about to let my brother's first meeting with one of his

favorite bands be anything other than awesome. "I see you all
got my memo and we're all up bright and early?"

"Jesus, Levi," Viper said. "Can you maybe lower your voice
about three million decibels? It's bad enough you made us get
up at the crack-ass of dawn after Kill's birthday, now you're
gonna be talking all loud and shit."

"It's noon. And I'm talking at a normal volume, so how
about you down some coffee and become human for me?" My
eyes fell to Slade, who was eyeing me and Liam with a
confused look on his face.

"Okay, so I know I drank a lot last night, but I'm totally
seeing two of you right now."

I rubbed the bridge of my nose. "You're not seeing double."
Moron. "I got you guys up because my brother and Imogen are
coming in today. I wanted you all decent to meet them, but
clearly that boat has sailed when it comes to Liam." I looked to
my brother. "I apologize for these guys who all drank too much
last night and—"

"It's fine," Liam said, shooting me a look that said *drop it.*

"You have a twin brother?" Jagger got to his feet as Killian
came back into the room to join his bandmates. "You didn't tell
us that."

I shrugged, not about to cop to the fact that I might've left
out that important detail. There was no way I was letting
Killian feel as though he had justification for trying to kiss the
wrong damn brother—*idiot.*

Jagger walked over to Liam and me, and except for the
bloodshot eyes, he looked as put together as ever. "Holy shit.
An *identical* twin," he said as he looked back and forth between
the two of us.

"Damn, it's almost uncanny. But I can totally tell you two
apart." Jagger pointed to Liam. "Liam has dimples when he
smiles, and Levi doesn't." When Liam nodded, I glared at
Killian, who was studying the carpet under his feet.

Good, let him feel ridiculous. How could he not tell the two of us apart? He should've known. He's kissed me, for God's sake.

Another knock at the door had Jagger backing away. "I'll get this one," he said. "Nice to meet you, Liam."

"Wait." Slade jumped to his feet with a surprising amount of energy for someone I'd thought was half-dead. "I'll come too."

Must be room service, I thought. Food was probably the only thing that would have them jumping up so damn fast, but as a female voice squealed, I realized it wasn't room service at the door after all, but Halo's sister, Imogen.

"Yo, Im! In here," Halo called out, shoving his sunglasses on top of his head.

As Imogen made her way inside, her long red waves trailing behind her, I couldn't help but notice the way Slade and Jagger flanked her in an almost protective way.

Oh shit. No. No, no, no, motherfucking no. I'd had my suspicions but had hoped to God I was just seeing things.

"Halo," she said, giving her brother a bear hug once he got to his feet to greet her. "I thought the flight over here would be unbearable, but it wasn't bad at all." She ruffled his hair. "You need a haircut."

"Nope. No, he doesn't," Viper said, causing Imogen to roll her eyes.

"So," she said, looking around the room. "Looks like you all partied hard last night. What were you celebrating? Jagger's many engagements?"

The way she said it sounded innocent and teasing enough, but she cut her eyes at Jagger.

"My what?" he said.

"Oh, I saw all those proposal signs on TV. How many did you say yes to?"

When Jagger began to sputter and Halo's eyes darted between Imogen and Jagger, I knew it was time to intervene.

"Since we're all here and in such fantastic moods," I said, "why don't we head down for lunch?"

"A greasy burger sounds like fucking heaven," Slade murmured, still standing too close to Imogen. I didn't know what was going on with those three, but they were *not* sitting together at lunch.

I sighed as everyone made their way out of Killian's suite and slung my arm around Liam's shoulders. "Welcome to Australia, baby bro. Sorry about the dramatics. They'll be fine once they get some food in their stomachs."

"Nah, they're great. But, uh..." He nodded at Killian and whispered, "Care to tell me what that was about?"

As if he knew we were talking about him, Killian looked over his shoulder, his eyes landing on mine, still apologetic, before turning away.

"Don't ask," I told my brother, shutting the door behind us. "Just don't even ask."

FOURTEEN

Killian

I'D FUCKED UP.

Nothing I said seemed to make any bit of difference to Levi, because apparently hitting on his twin brother I hadn't even known existed was too unforgivable a crime, one punishable by silence for the foreseeable future. He ignored me at lunch, on the flight to Sydney, at dinner last night after getting some sightseeing in.

For fuck's sake.

To me, the whole thing was laughable. Obviously I hadn't done it on purpose, and now that I'd met Liam—who seemed to be the polar opposite of Levi, in looks and personality—it sure as hell wouldn't be a mistake I'd make again. Unlike his twin, Liam had laughed off our interaction, though I suspected he was curious as to why I'd been coming on to his brother the way I had.

There was only one thing I could do at this point to get Levi's attention back on me, and not in the "shooting daggers into my eyeballs" kind of way. He'd fucking hate it at first, which was why I'd resorted to being a sneaky bastard, but if things went my way, he'd appreciate the gesture later.

Maybe.

Lounging against the padded seat at the front of the boat I'd rented for a few hours, I kicked my legs up on the seat across from me and checked the time. Our usually punctual band manager would be here soon, so while I waited, I closed my eyes and soaked in the sun's warm rays.

It wasn't long before I heard footsteps on the dock and opened my eyes as Levi came to a stop in front of the boat. Squinting up at him, I shielded my eyes and noted the pissed-off expression that seemed to be a permanent fixture on his face for the last twenty-four hours. He'd dressed as casually as he ever seemed to, a pair of sea-green shorts and a white linen shirt showcasing his tanned skin, loafers on his feet.

Gorgeous. The man was too fucking gorgeous for his own good, even when he was scowling.

Levi scanned the boat, along with the others nearby, and even with his sunglasses on, I could feel the way his eyes narrowed on me. "What is this?"

"An EasyRider 069," I said, stroking the edge of the rail. "With a number like that, I couldn't resist."

"Why doesn't that surprise me?" he muttered, and then sighed. "I was under the impression everyone was coming."

I shrugged. "Maybe they're running late."

"There aren't enough seats. The boat looks like it barely holds four people."

"Five, actually." I got to my feet and pulled the keys from my pocket. "If you're coming, get in."

Moving behind the wheel, I looked back to see Levi still standing on the dock, his arms crossed.

"Tell me you didn't rent this for the two of us," he said.

"I didn't rent this for the two of us." It wasn't a lie if he told me to say it.

He shook his head. "I don't believe you. I think you manipulated me into coming down here so I'll talk to you."

Well, he technically *was* talking to me, so my plan had worked already. "Maybe I did, maybe I didn't."

"This is some bullshit." Levi turned around and started back up the dock until I called out for him to stop.

"Levi, you're already here—

"Thanks to you—"

"—so you may as well get in."

He strolled back to the boat. "Yeah? So I can waste even more of my day listening to your lame-ass excuses?" He snorted. "No thanks."

"Levi." I sighed, clenching my hands around the wheel as I struggled for patience. The guy was going to drive me out of my mind, and at this point, I didn't know whether I wanted to spend the day with him or pitch him overboard. "Look, you don't have to talk to me. You just have to get in the boat with me."

Levi pushed his sunglasses up on top of his head and crouched down so we were at eye level. "You sure you have the right brother? Maybe you meant to call Liam."

"Oh, give it up, for fuck's sake," I said, rolling my eyes as I walked back toward the front of the boat. "You know better."

"Do I?"

"Yes. And if you don't know now, you will once you *get in the boat.*"

"Ahh, so I'm right? It's just you and me, stuck together in the middle of the harbor so that unless I want to take a dive, I can't escape."

"Oh, Levi," I practically purred, holding his gaze as I reached up to finger his shirt, pulling him closer until I could feel his warm breath against my lips. "Why would you ever want to escape?"

His eyes bored into mine, jaw set, but I could see the way he swallowed, like he wanted exactly what I was ready to give him but his pride wouldn't allow him to acquiesce so easily.

It was a long minute before he spoke again.

"You're in my way," he said quietly.

I blinked, wondering if I'd heard him correctly. I still had a hold of his shirt, and the thought crossed my mind that if I let go, he'd take off.

Choosing to believe he wanted to stay, I dropped my hand and took a step back.

Levi stared at me for a long moment, and then ran his hand through his hair. "Don't make me regret this," he said, before stepping down into the boat.

Turning away before he could see the smile on my face, I headed back to the driver's seat and started up the engine.

"Do me a favor." I nodded toward where the boat was attached by a rope to the dock. "Untie the rope from the piling so we can head out."

Levi made quick work of the rope, and as I backed us away from the pier, he took a seat in the front, as far away from me as possible. It didn't matter, though—there was no escaping me now.

FIFTEEN

Levi

I'M WEAK. SO damn weak when it comes to Killian. That was my only excuse for how I'd ended up sitting at the front of this damn boat with the wind in my hair, the sun on my face, and the fresh, salty spray from the harbor misting over my skin.

Well, that, and it was a gorgeous day, and even with how annoyed I was at the man standing behind the wheel, I wasn't about to pass up on the opportunity to see the Sydney Harbor from the water.

With my sunglasses in place, I made it a point to turn my back on Killian and watch the boats, ferries, and scenery we were passing by, determined to keep my distance even though he'd managed to corner me on a boat no bigger than the bathroom back in my hotel suite.

Still annoyed at having walked up on Killian putting the moves on my brother, I'd tried my hardest to avoid him at all costs since then, only to find myself within the same vicinity of the gorgeous bastard at every turn I made.

It was beyond irritating, not to mention frustrating, because even though I was actively trying to avoid him, every single part of me wanted to get closer. *I am weak.*

As the boat sped through the water, I tried my hardest not to show I was white-knuckling the railing in front of me, trusting that Killian wouldn't put his or my life in danger, but of course he drove like a bat out of hell.

Like any self-respecting rock star, Killian liked to work hard and play even harder. It was something I'd been more than aware of when I signed on as their manager. He was single and liked to mingle—a lot. But I had to admit, over the past several months, any playing Killian had done must've taken place on the down-low, because I hadn't heard anything when it came to his...extracurricular escapades, and thank God for that.

Sneaking a look over my shoulder, I let my shaded eyes trail down Killian's loose white button-up, to his navy board shorts, tanned, muscled calves, and the flip-flops he'd slipped on to finish off the sexy/casual vibe he had going on.

Ugh. If he wasn't so damn sexy, ignoring him would be so much easier.

"It feels good out here today, doesn't it?"

Acting as though I wasn't just checking him out, I made a point of tilting my face up in Killian's direction and shrugged. "I suppose. But I could've enjoyed the weather just as easily from my balcony."

Killian snorted. "Oh, come on. You can't tell me your balcony would've felt half as good as it does out here. The wind, the sun, the surf... Not to mention these spectacular views."

He had a point. The views out here were pretty spectacular, and so was my captain.

No. No, no. You are not going there. Squash that thought right now.

"The views *are* pretty hard to beat."

Killian tipped his sunglasses down, his blue eyes sweeping over me. "I couldn't agree more."

I scoffed. "Just can't help yourself, can you?" When Killian arched a brow, I added, "The flirting. The teasing. It comes so easy to you. Almost as easy as breathing."

As I went to turn away, Killian said, "No. Uh ah. You don't get to do that here. You want to have a go at me, then come on. No one else is here. Bring it on."

I wasn't sure why, but Killian's irritated tone had my temper rising. I hadn't meant to start a fight with him. In fact, I'd meant to ignore him for as long as I possibly could. But now that he'd thrown down the gauntlet, the hell if I was about to back down.

"All right," I said, getting to my feet and half shuffling, half stumbling to where he stood. I gripped one of the rails by the wheel and windshield protecting the controls and let him have it.

"To start with, I told you the first time we kissed it could go no further than that, and *you*"—I jabbed at his arm—"didn't listen. Instead, you continue to come on to me time after time, and I have been trying to be professional and ignore you. But you are making it very hard."

As soon as the word left my mouth and Killian's lips curved, I said, "Don't even think about making a joke out of that."

Killian shook his head, innocent as can be, which was *not* innocent at all. So before he could open his mouth and distract me, I continued.

"Second." I held my middle finger up next to my pointer. "Just when I had everything worked out, compartmentalized, you were in your lane and I was in mine, we get to Australia and you had to go and drop your damn robe, showing all of"— I waved my hand in his general direction—"*this* off, making it close to impossible to erase it from my fucking mind. And then, as if all of that isn't bad enough, I had to see you hitting on my brother after you'd rubbed all over me the night before. *You*. Are the most frustrating human being I have ever met."

As I stopped to take a breath, I tried to think if there was anything I had missed, and then Killian leaned in close to me and said, "In other words, you're just as hot for me as I am for you. Hmm, can't tell you how long I've waited for you to admit that."

My mouth fell open. Of course that was all he'd taken away from what I'd said. "I didn't admit that."

As Killian directed the boat into a small bay and slowed, he angled his body to mine and again reached out to finger my shirt, rubbing his fingertip back and forth over the button.

"Yeah, you did. I mean, it's not like you haven't already told me. But it's nice to hear when you're sober—"

I wrapped my fingers around his wrist, halting him. "Wait a second. What do you mean *when I'm sober*?"

SIXTEEN

Killian

OF COURSE LEVI didn't remember what he'd said to me on the dance floor the night of my birthday. I hadn't expected him to, and honestly, even if he had remembered, I doubted he'd admit it without prompting.

With his hand around my wrist, he asked again, "What do you mean when I'm sober? Did I say something?"

I slid my finger in between the buttons on his shirt, feeling the warmth of his chest. "You said I was the one who excited you." Flipping open one of the buttons, I leaned in close and said, "Always."

Levi trembled slightly, the fury in his eyes from seconds ago morphing into something altogether different—something passionate, fierce.

"Is that true?" I said as the warm breeze kicked up from the water and ruffled open Levi's shirt. As the soft linen parted, it revealed a smooth, tanned strip of his skin, and there was nothing I wanted more than to kiss and lick my way down it. "Am I the one you want?"

Levi flexed his fingers around my wrist, and I could see his pulse thrumming at the base of his throat. *Fuck*, that was such a turn-on. "I really said that?"

"You did. So? Truth or lie?"

Levi swallowed, and for the first time ever, I thought I detected nerves on my sexy manager. "Truth. But—"

"Uh ah," I said, placing a finger to his lips. "No buts. You add that and it takes away from the major victory I feel I just accomplished here."

Levi's lips curved under my finger, and when the smile reached his eyes, my heart close to stopped. The guy was fucking beautiful, and this was the first time he'd aimed a genuine smile my way in…weeks.

"I'm gonna go ahead and stop here for a bit if that works for you. The plan was to take you somewhere for lunch, but before we get there, I think maybe we should"—when Levi's eyes fell to my lips, I smirked—"talk."

I removed my hands from the tempting man in front of me, and as I was about to turn away to guide the boat further into the small bay, Levi took his sunglasses off, eyeing me closely.

"This won't change anything, Killian. No matter how many talks we have, you're still you and I'm still me."

"Wow, that's, like…genius, Levi."

"Oh, shut up," he said. "You know what I mean."

I glanced his way and could tell by the way he was fidgeting with his sunglasses that the nerves from a minute ago were still there, even if he had been able to shove them back behind his manager's mask for now.

"I don't, actually. If anything, the fact that it *is* you and it *is* me is exactly why that should change things. We want the same thing here, Levi."

As I drew the boat to a stop and cut the engine, I turned to face him as Levi asked, "And that is?"

"Each other."

Levi groaned and brought his hands up to his face as the boat gently bobbed in the calm waters. "You are so…so…"

"Sexy?"

Levi dropped his hands and pinned me with a look that made my cock jerk inside my shorts, although I didn't think that was his intention.

"I was thinking more like stubborn or persistent."

"Or charming and good-looking."

Levi chuckled and put his glasses back on. "You are a charming bastard, I'll give you that."

"See? That's my second victory for the day—three and I'm on a roll. Want to just tell me you can't wait to see me naked again? I won't tell anyone you gave in so fast."

"No," Levi said, and turned to walk back up to the front of the boat. Then he took a seat so he was facing me. "I'm not going to make it that easy on you."

I stopped directly in front of him in the narrow bow. "How about hard? Because I have to tell you, Levi, you're really good at making me that."

Levi's eyes dropped to the hard-on I had no hope of hiding. "I think you should go and sit over there." He pointed to the seats on the starboard side, and I chuckled.

"I mean, if you can't keep your hands to yourself, I can—"

"Oh my God. You're delusional."

"And you're really fucking hot when you get all…blustery like this."

"Blustery?" Levi said, as I took a seat where he'd suggested. But I made sure to stretch my legs out in front of me and hook my feet around his. "I don't get blustery."

"Okay, how about wound up? Is that a better way to say it? This fiery side of you pushes all my buttons."

Levi's mouth fell open, and just when I thought he was about to lob a retort my way, he started to chuckle. The sound was raspy and sexy, and then he leaned back against the rails and put his palms up. "Okay. Okay. Shit. I give in. You're clearly on a mission today, and"—he looked around at the secluded spot I'd anchored us—"if you want to say my *practical business* side turns you on, who am I to stop you? I'm a catch; you'd be lucky to have me."

Ah, no kidding. I wasn't a fucking moron. I'd be hella lucky to have any part of Levi, and I wasn't about to pass up the opportunity to plead my case now that I had him alone and he seemed willing to listen.

"But here's the problem, as my practical business mind sees it. You're an international rock god with millions of fans wanting to climb in your bed at any given hour of any given day, and I don't want to climb over them on my way out of it. This isn't my first rodeo, Killian—I've been in this business for years. And just because you make my dick hard and my brain a little fuzzy, doesn't mean I'm going to throw all of my rules and common sense out the window." Levi paused and took in a deep breath before blowing it out. "Even if you are ridiculously attractive."

As Levi's words ran through my mind, I studied him. "Levi?" I took my sunglasses off to be sure he could see that what I was about to say was the God's honest truth.

"When are you going to understand that I don't want that anymore? I don't want them. I've also been in this business for years, and never have I wanted anything other than what you just described. But with you? Damn, Levi. From the second I set eyes on you, there's been no one else. And if you stopped fighting me so hard at every turn, you just might see that."

SEVENTEEN

Levi

JESUS. WHEN KILLIAN turned his full attention on you, it was deadly. Combine that with the words coming out of his mouth, and I was surprised I hadn't fallen out of the damn seat.

His blue eyes implored me to believe him, and I wanted to, but something he said had a red flag waving in front of me.

"From the second you laid eyes on me...no one else? Seriously?" I found that hard—no, impossible—to believe. "You're telling me you haven't been with anyone for—"

"Months."

I let that sink in for a minute before I chuckled, shaking my head. "Right. You almost had me."

"You think I'm joking?" He sat back, resting his arms along the rail, his foot still hooked behind mine. "It's been about...six months, five days, and probably a handful of hours, if we're being *really* specific."

My mouth fell open. "What the... But—"

"But what? Have you seen me with anyone?"

"Well, no—"

"Caught me looking at anyone the way I look at you?"

He was out of his damn mind. "Killian, that's fucking crazy."

"Yes. It is. But I know you're worth it."

I couldn't breathe. Couldn't speak. Couldn't do anything but stare in complete and utter shock.

Killian was dead serious, of that I had no doubt, not anymore, but what the hell was I supposed to do with that information? I'd never been one to go with my emotions over logic, but I couldn't deny Killian was making it difficult not to say fuck it and throw caution to the wind.

"Worth it," I repeated to myself quietly. Yeah, I was worth it. I had enough self-respect and confidence to know that much, and Killian was a smart man to recognize a good thing when he saw it. It wasn't like I couldn't say the same thing about him, but—

"I see you every day. I watch how you are with people, how they react to you. There's just something about you, Levi. Something that makes me want to be around you. Makes me want to be *with* you."

I tried to stop the smile that pulled at my lips. Who knew Killian was such a sweet talker? His words were enough to melt even my steel heart, though I'd be damned if I showed it.

"Right," I said. "So this isn't just about sex. You're not looking to win some kind of challenge here."

Killian gave me a *fuckin' really?* look. "Uh, no. I would've lost months ago."

"And you want this thing between us to be...more."

"Is it finally sinking into that stubborn head of yours?"

I smiled at the exasperation in his voice but it soon fell. "I can't promise you more, Killian."

"Then maybe you can promise to stop overthinking this. I don't need a declaration of fucking love here; I just want to give this thing between us a chance. You think you can do that?"

Could I? Turn my brain off, simple as that?

With a sigh, I mimicked Killian's position, leaning back against the seat and laying my arms out over the rail. "You mentioned lunch. How about we start there?"

A brilliant smile lit up Killian's face as he got to his feet and made quick work of pulling up anchor. Then he moved in behind the wheel and started up the boat—

Well, tried to start up the boat.

With a frown marring his forehead, Killian took the key out and reinserted it, trying again, but there was no sound except the light sputtering of a failing engine.

"Shit." As he tried to get the boat cranked, I headed to the rear, only to see a wisp of smoke flowing out from the motor.

"Uh, Killian?" I glanced over my shoulder and nodded at the rising smoke. "I think we have a problem."

"Motherfucker—" Killian rushed past me to get a good look at what was happening, and then he let out a long string of curses.

"Oh come on," I said, sidling up beside him. "Don't tell me you didn't plan to get me all alone and then get us conveniently stranded."

Killian gave me a side-eye as he groaned. "I wish I could take credit, but no. Fuck."

"That's too bad. I don't suppose they have a coast guard in Australia..." I pulled my cell out of my shorts pocket and searched boat rescue in Sydney Harbor, and when several options came up, I hit the number for the first company. As I waited for the line to connect, I glanced back at Killian. "Looks like you owe me more than lunch now."

EIGHTEEN

Levi

KILLIAN MICHAELS. WOW. For the past few months, I'd put up a gallant effort in resisting his charms, but this afternoon, he'd turned out to be a revelation. Not in the sense that he was smooth as whiskey, sexy as sin, and pretty much everything I could ever want in a man. But in the way that *he* apparently felt the same exact way about me.

I mean, I wasn't blind—I'd known that Killian was interested in me. I'd felt it in every nerve of my body whenever he looked my way. But when he'd flat-out confessed to waiting months for a chance to *have* me? Holy shit. Nothing could've shocked me more.

Killian could have anyone. Literally *anyone* he wanted. Yet he'd rejected all of those offers for a chance at a date with me. As if that wasn't enough of a stroke to my ego, the way he was currently staring at me from across the table added enough pressure to make sure my dick felt it too. I shifted on the seat, and a confident smile stretched across Killian's full lips. I automatically remembered the way they'd felt against mine, and couldn't wait to feel them again.

"Will this table be okay, Mr. Michaels?" When we'd arrived,

Killian had asked the hostess for the most private table they had, and while I knew it was so he wouldn't get hounded all night, a part of me also liked to think it was because he didn't want anyone interrupting our time together.

Killian kept his eyes on me as his feet found mine under the table, then he nodded. "This is absolutely perfect."

Jesus. That unwavering focus? That complete and total attention he was aiming my way? It was potent as hell, and while I'd always known if I gave in to Killian I was going to have a hard time keeping the upper hand, I didn't expect it to happen five minutes into dinner.

It was as though the second we'd stepped off the boat and our maritime adventure was behind us, Killian switched from the embarrassed sea captain back to the charming, confident rock star I found nearly impossible to resist.

As the hostess hurried off to find our waiter, Killian leaned forward in his chair and rested his arms on the table. With his face sun-kissed from our...extended afternoon on the bay, Killian's thick hair was swept back from his face, and the flickering candle on the table only enhanced his striking features. He'd never looked more attractive.

"What are you thinking about?" Killian's honey-toned voice floated across the air and wrapped around me.

"What makes you so sure I'm thinking about something?"

Killian knowingly smirked. "You have this look in your eye..."

"And what look's that?"

"Hmm." Killian pursed his lips and rubbed a finger over them, and if his goal was to draw my attention there, he succeeded. "I'm still deciding, but it's something...hot."

He wasn't wrong. He *was* hot. But deciding to play with him a little now that I had the freedom to, I said, "Sure you aren't talking about what *you're* thinking?"

Killian chuckled and sat back in his seat, his eyes roving

over as much of me that he could see. "I mean, that's a given. I haven't exactly made it a secret that I want you."

"No," I said, reaching for the menu. "You haven't."

Killian eyed me as I flipped it open and made a valiant effort to read the items on the page. "*Sooo*? What are you thinking about?"

I glanced over the top of the laminated list, and as I drank in the stubble lining his strong jaw, I finally gave him what he was asking for—an honest reaction. "I'm thinking about all of the things I'd do to you—if I wanted to."

Killian's mouth fell open, that answer clearly not what he'd been expecting. But he quickly regrouped. "Such as?"

His question was raspy, and my cock kicked in response. Up until now, I'd either been fending Killian off or fighting my own responses. But even though I'd finally given myself permission to enjoy tonight, to enjoy him, I wasn't about to lay it all out there…yet.

"If you think I'm about to give up all my secrets *before* you buy me dinner, you don't know me at all. Oh, wait, you don't really know me, do you? You didn't even know I had a—"

"I know, I know, a twin brother. Are you ever going to let me live that down?"

I aimed a winning smile his way. "Just pointing out some important facts."

"Fair enough." Killian picked up his menu and sat back in his seat, and it was all I could do to keep the smirk from my lips.

Killian stared at the options in front of him and frowned, and not a second later he put the menu back on the table and said, "Okay, then, what else don't I know about you?"

I lost the battle then. I knew the expression on my face now read one thing and one thing only—smug. I had one of the biggest rock stars on the planet looking at me as though he were waiting for me to impart state secrets to him, and that kind of attention was intoxicating.

Killian was intoxicating

"All of the good things," I said. "And by that I mean the very *bad* things. The kind of things I shouldn't talk about at work or…with a client."

Killian's eyes darkened, and just as he was about to respond, our waiter sidled up to the table.

"Good evening. My name's David and I'll be your waiter for the night. Are you ready to order?"

When Killian shook his head, I looked up at David and smiled. "Sorry, we're not quite ready yet. Could you give us a few more minutes?"

"Of course, just signal me when you're ready."

"Will do," I said, and when David walked away and I returned my attention to Killian, my breath all but caught in my throat.

Killian had leaned across the table toward me, and the frustration from a moment ago had now been replaced with a crackling energy. Those blue eyes were roaming over my face, and when they finally came up to lock on mine, my heart stuttered.

"Just to clarify," Killian said in a raspy voice that did absolutely nothing to help the ache between my thighs, "how bad is bad? You see, I have a very vivid imagination, and if you don't expand on that, who knows where my mind will go."

Oh, I had a pretty good idea where his mind would go, and that was exactly the problem. When I got around Killian, I lost focus. Well, focus on work, anyway, and that was the very reason getting involved was a terrible idea. A super-hot one that would most certainly satisfy the both of us many times over, but terrible just the same.

I had rules for a reason, and if ever there was a time to remember that, it was now.

I shrugged. "Bad enough that if you and I were to do something, and then it all ended up on its ass, the only way I'd ever feel comfortable again would be to quit."

"What?" Killian said, and sat back in his seat. "That's crazy."

"That's the truth. Let's say we act on this…"

"Hot-as-fuck chemistry?"

That about summed it up. "Yes. Let's say we act on this chemistry and we spend six months in each other's beds—then things end. How would you ever listen to me again, and take my advice seriously as opposed to personal? The answer is: you wouldn't."

A heavy silence settled between us as Killian stared at me as though I'd lost my mind. And maybe I had. I was sitting at dinner with the sexiest man I'd ever known and was doing my best to stop him from looking at me as though he wanted to get me somewhere naked, now.

I'd definitely lost my mind.

"Okay, first off," Killian said. "You have us broken up and we haven't even finished our first date yet."

"This isn't a date." I knew that was a lie, even as I was saying it.

"It is so a damn date. It's just the two of us, there's a candle on the table, and we're talking about you being in my bed."

"Actually, we were talking about me *not* being there after we broke up."

"In your shitty hypothetical, maybe. Want to hear my version of that story?"

No was my immediate thought, because I knew it would be too tempting. But when I didn't immediately answer, Killian kept talking.

"In my version of that story," he said, and then stretched one of his legs out to hook his foot around my ankle, much like he had back on the boat, "we have a kickass date tonight. I take you back to the hotel. I show you just how *hot* this chemistry is between us, and you stop overthinking everything."

As I stared into Killian's eyes, I could see that he really believed what he was saying—that it would be easy as that for us to hook up, share a bed, and let things run their course.

But I knew better. I'd been there, done that. Hence the rules.

"I wish it could be that easy," I said, and meant it. There was nothing I wanted more than to go back to my hotel room with Killian. "But it's not. You have to see that."

Killian picked his menu up. "All I see is a man who keeps denying himself what he clearly wants. Why, Levi? And don't give me that bullshit professional answer of yours. Tell me the truth."

I licked my suddenly dry lips and knew I needed to just tell him about my past. It wasn't as though Killian would fire me once he found out. But at the same time, I hated that I had to share this mistake with him. That I had to admit how naive I'd once been. Even now I still found the whole thing...humiliating.

"Okay, I'll tell you. But then you have to promise to let it go."

"No way. That's not how this works."

"Professional dater, are you?"

"Actually, I've never been on a real date before. You're my first."

I studied Killian's serious expression. "What about before me? I know you saw people."

Killian shrugged, "All casual fu—"

I chuckled. "All casual fucks, huh?"

"Geez, Levi, I was trying to be polite."

"Since when?"

Killian leaned forward, and the candlelight flickered over his skin, adding to his stunning looks. "Since tonight. I'm trying to impress you."

I grinned. "Is that right?"

"It is… So?"

As I stared into his twinkling blue eyes, I forgot about my rules and all the reasons I had them. "So what?"

The smile that appeared was full of sin and sex. "Are you impressed?"

God, I was in so much trouble here. If I was smart, I'd demand to be taken back to the hotel—now. But I wasn't. And I didn't. "Yes. But—"

"No buts." Killian tongued his lower lip. "But let's order. The quicker we do that, the quicker you can tell me why you keep saying no when your eyes are screaming yes."

I swallowed back my automatic denial as Killian raised his hand, and before I knew it, David was taking our orders.

If someone had asked me what I had decided on to eat right then, I couldn't have told them. I was too busy trying to work out how to explain my past to Killian without making myself sound like a fool. I might have been young and dumb back then, but I still had my pride, and I didn't want him to see me as anything other than fucking perfect. Something I clearly wasn't in the story I had to tell.

As if he could read my mind, Killian sat back in his seat, adopting the cool and casual disposition he was so well known for, and waited for me to talk—damn it.

There was no getting out of this. I knew I was stubborn, but over the last few months Killian had definitely given me a run for my money. Still was, judging by the silence that was lingering between us.

"My rules," I started, and then reached for the glass of Pinot Noir in front of me, knowing I'd need a drink sooner rather than later. "They're there for a reason, Killian. I didn't just make them up when I agreed to manage Fallen Angel."

Killian rested a hand on the table and smoothed his fingers over the cloth. He had nice hands, big, strong fingers, and the longer I sat there looking at them, the more I realized I wanted to feel them on me—every single part of me —tonight.

But we weren't there yet, and we might never be.

"Okay," Killian said. "So what happened?" When I stared at him, trying to find the right words to say, Killian touched his fingers to mine. "Who broke your heart, Levi?"

I blinked at him, my mind completely blown that he'd zeroed in so quickly on what was happening here, but then again, no one could accuse Killian of being stupid.

"Tell me, so I can go and kick his ass."

My lips twitched. "You almost sound serious."

"I am." Killian's eyes twinkled with mischief. "Just give me his name, and I'll take care of him." Killian paused. "I assume it *was* a him?"

I snorted. "Of course it was a him."

"Ah ha! So that is the reason for these strict-ass rules of yours. Some douchebag did break your heart."

I let out a sigh and slipped my hand away from his to rub it over my face. *Here goes nothing.* "Not so much my heart. More my pride. My ego."

As I was about to launch into the whole sordid affair, David appeared with two plates and slid them onto the table in front of us.

Oh, what do you know, I'd ordered the clam, shrimp, and chorizo pasta.

As David disappeared, I reached for my napkin, placed it over my lap, and then carefully laid out my utensils. When I looked up, I found Killian grinning at me. "What?"

"I was just thinking how put together you are. How buttoned up and proper. With the napkin and the perfect manners."

"Oh yeah?"

"Mhmm. Makes me want to ruffle your feathers. Makes me

so fucking curious about how you are when you finally give in and let go."

With him, I'd be insatiable. I already knew that.

I loved sex, everything about it. From the racing pulse, to the sweaty skin, to the push and pull that I knew I'd have with Killian. As I stared into his knowing eyes, I was more than aware that the man across from me would be the best sex of my life.

"That's part of the problem," I said, and stabbed at one of the shrimp.

"What is?"

"You make me want to forget about everything but…"

"But?"

"But finding a bed and getting in it with you."

"I don't see a problem with that."

"And all I can see *are* problems with that. I've been here before, Killian. Back when I first started. And I promised myself I'd never go there again."

Killian's jaw twitched, and I wasn't sure if it was frustration over me again denying him, or over the thought of me in bed with someone else. I quickly had my answer.

"So you're denying the both of us because of some asshole you let into your bed years ago? I don't know who this guy is, but I really fucking hate him." Killian reached for his Heineken and took a swig. "I'm not him, you know."

"I know."

"Do you? Because it doesn't sound like you do." Killian picked up his fork and speared a piece of steak on his plate. "Sounds like you're punishing me for something he did."

"By not sleeping with you? Come on, Killian—"

"No, you come on, Levi. That night back in Atlanta?" Killian paused, his eyes roaming over my face, searching for something, but I wasn't sure what. "It was the best night of my life. Fallen Angel had just kicked ass and we knew we had something really special going on again. But it was what came *after* that made that night so fucking amazing—you."

I let out a shaky sigh. This was hopeless, it was like butting heads with a bull. A very persistent, very persuasive bull.

"You're right," I said. "That night was amazing. That kiss, nothing short of spectacular. And if I give in and end up in your bed, it's those things that tell me I'm going to get hurt. The same way I have been before."

"Levi..." Killian put his fork down and reached for my hand.

"You want the dirty details?" I said, looking him directly in the eye. "You want to know why I have rules? Why I don't fuck around with my clients?"

Killian said nothing, and I took that as a resounding yes.

"When I first started, I interned with Vista Records and was working with The Nothing. I was young, naive, and more than a little green, so you can imagine how flattered I was when Jonny took a special interest in me."

"Wait a fucking minute."

Killian's interruption wasn't all that unexpected. I'd known he and the other guys from TBD were pretty close with The Nothing, which was why I'd tried to keep this humiliating piece of my past far, *far* away from my current place of employment.

"You're telling me that you and Jonny were together?"

I winced at the disgust in Killian's voice but knew it wasn't for me.

"*Together* is too kind a term for what he reduced it to."

"That motherfucker."

Choosing not to address that, I forged ahead, like ripping off a Band-Aid. "They were hot and new on the scene. I got wrapped up in the thrill of working so close to someone I admired, and when he invited me up to his room for a drink one night, I thought, where's the harm in that?"

Killian had stopped eating his meal and was watching me with an intensity I'd never felt from him before. He was fuming mad, but not at me, at the situation, at the one who wasn't there for him to yell at.

"What happened?" Killian said between clenched teeth. "Did he hurt you?"

The answer was no, not physically, and thank God for that. I wasn't quite sure what Killian would do if the answer had been yes.

"We were together for about five months. I thought we were one thing—a couple working out the best way to navigate this new thing between us—but the day they were set to leave on their first international tour, I was let go from the internship. A decision, I was told, that was made by the band."

Killian's hand fisted into a ball on the tablecloth, his attention one hundred percent on me.

"I later found out that Jonny told them I was obsessed with him. That I wouldn't leave him alone even though he'd ended things." I paused and lowered my eyes to the meal in front of me, thinking about that for a second. "Which I guess is true, in a way, because I kept calling him. Because I had no clue he wanted out."

When silence was all that met my ears, I raised my eyes to see Killian looking at me in a way that made my heart skip all over itself.

"Pretty stupid, huh?"

Killian's eyes softened, and my pulse began to race. "If you mean him, then yes, he's really fucking stupid. But everyone who meets Jonny knows that. So why don't we look at your experience in a new light? One where you dodged a fucking bullet, and are now sitting at dinner with the most handsome, charming bastard you've ever met in your life."

I shook my head but grinned. "Is that right?"

"Damn right it is. And Levi?"

As I spun my fork in my pasta, I met Killian's gaze head-on. "Yeah?"

"I'm not stupid, and I know what's in front of me, and I'm going to do everything in my power to make you realize that some rules are worth breaking."

NINETEEN

Killian

_____

FUCK JONNY.

I'D always had a bad feeling about that irritating asshole. But after hearing what he'd done to Levi, I wanted to track him down and beat the hell out of him.

What a selfish piece of shit. He could've very well ended Levi's career with the bullshit move he'd made. But due to Levi's determination and grit, he'd proven to the world—and no doubt himself—that he was more than some rock star's quick fuck. He'd gone on to become one of the top managers in the industry, and now managed the biggest rock band in the world, the biggest fuck you he could've ever given to Jonny, and hell if that didn't make him all the more appealing.

I looked at Levi finishing off his dessert, and wondered what he was thinking about. After he'd spilled his guts, Levi had gone about eating his meal quietly, as though reflecting on everything he'd just confessed to.

I knew this had to have been difficult for him; Levi was never one to act anything other than confident and self-assured. But right now he appeared more vulnerable than I'd ever seen him before, and I wanted him to know that with me, he never had to feel anything other than safe.

"How's your dessert?"

Levi raised his eyes to meet mine, and when a smile slowly curved his lips, my heart began to race. Jesus, the man was unbelievably beautiful. I mean, I'd always thought he was sexy, but when he dropped the scowl and looked at me the way he was now—as though he were actually *enjoying* my company—I was pretty sure I'd get on my knees and beg him for date two if he tried to deny me.

"It's delicious. The entire meal was."

"Agreed. I can see why this place came so highly recommended."

Levi scooped up another spoonful of pavlova. "Were you asking around?"

"Maybe. I couldn't exactly steal you away and then take you to McDonald's for lunch, could I?"

"Ah, we're back to you trying to impress me, huh?" Levi slipped the spoon between the lips I wanted to kiss, and when he dragged it free all nice and clean, I reached beneath the table to readjust myself.

Levi swallowed his sweet treat, and I noticed a spot of cream on the corner of his lips and crooked my finger at him. When he leaned across the table, I swiped the cream off with my thumb and licked it clean.

"Always. I swear, everything I do lately is to impress you." Levi's lips parted, and if we hadn't been in such a public place, I would've lowered my mouth to his and taken the kiss it was clear we both wanted. "Levi?"

Levi blinked slowly, and it pleased the hell out of me when he swayed toward me.

"Yes?"

"Thank you for telling me about Jonny."

"Odd thing to thank me for."

"Well, now it all makes more sense to me. I understand why you're hesitant to trust me."

Levi licked his lips, and damn, I would've given away everything I owned right then to follow his tongue with mine.

"It's not that I don't trust you—"

"Yes, it is," I said. "And who could blame you? Jonny was a total dick, and me? I've never had a relationship in my life."

Levi's eyes widened. "Never? You mean, you weren't joking earlier about the casual—"

"Hookups?" I interjected, not wanting him to think about the fact that he had once been a casual fuck to someone. "No. I wasn't joking. But I've always been very clear up front. I've never been with someone more than one night, and, well, no one's ever left my bed anything other than...pleased."

Levi shook his head, and the soft chuckle that left him made me grin.

"You're extremely arrogant," he said, but there was no malice behind the words. In fact, he sounded as though he liked my confidence a hell of a lot.

"So are you, just in different ways. It's one of the things that's so damn attractive about you."

"Killian..."

"About these rules of yours."

"Yes?"

"What was the first one again?"

Levi arched an eyebrow. "Don't sleep with your client."

I nodded and pursed my lips. "That's what I thought. But if I'm honest, sleeping wasn't really high on my list of things to do with you. So if it makes you feel better, we can cross that one off right now."

Levi scoffed. "You and I both know I mean don't have *sex* with a client."

I wasn't sure why, but hearing him lump me in with Jonny made my stomach twist. "And is that all I am to you? A client?"

"Killian," he said, shaking his head. "I not only have to think about my career—I have to think about yours too. So, yes, I think of you as a client because I'm your manager. That's my job. But God help me, I can't stop imagining…"

"What?" I said, my voice whisper soft as I desperately grabbed that opening with both hands. "You can't stop imagining *what*, Levi?"

With his eyes locked on mine, Levi rubbed his fingers across his lips. "I can't stop imagining what it would be like to be *more* than that with you."

The little blood that was left in my head rushed directly south at the fevered look in Levi's eyes, and without a word, I pushed back from the table and got to my feet. I reached into the pocket of my shorts and pulled my wallet free, and after throwing a couple of hundred-dollar bills on the table, I stopped beside Levi, who was looking up at me with wide eyes full of desire and…hesitation.

"What's rule three?" I said, and thanked God the shirt I was wearing fell far enough past the zipper of my shorts to keep me decent.

Levi got to his feet, and when we were face to face, his eyes fell to my mouth. "Never break rules one and two."

THE TRIP BACK to our hotel was made in silence. But unlike the comfortable quiet we'd experienced throughout dinner, this time the air was full of tension. I was highly aware of every move Levi made. When he stretched his legs, first the left then the right. When he bit down on his lower lip. When he smiled at something the Uber driver said. Every single thing he did made me want to reach over and touch him.

Instead, I sat beside him in the back of the car and thought back to what Levi had told me at dinner. I knew he was worried about what had happened in the past, and now that I understood his hesitation, the last thing I wanted him to think was that I was after a quick fuck.

Every now and then I would catch Levi looking in my direction, and whenever I met his gaze, he aimed a knowing smile my way, as though he knew how difficult I was finding it to keep my hands to myself. Because it was. And now I wasn't sure what I was supposed to do about it.

When we finally reached the hotel and made our way up to the top floor, I kept my hands jammed in my pockets. The last thing I needed was for a fan or one of the guys to see us acting any way other than normal, spooking Levi into re-erecting all his walls.

Levi's suite was the first off the elevator, mine was two more down, and when he stopped in front of his door, he looked at me and said, "Thank you for today."

Looking up and down the hall, I made sure the coast was clear and took a step closer to him. "So... I'm not in trouble for kidnapping you?"

Levi chuckled. "So you admit it? You did kidnap me today."

I placed a hand on the door by his head and nodded. "Oh yeah, I totally kidnapped you."

Levi raised a hand to my chest, and when I placed my other one over the top of his, he sighed. "Killian."

"Levi," I whispered over the top of his lips. "I'm gonna make you break your rules with me."

Levi clenched the material covering my chest. "That's probably not a good idea."

I grazed my lips over his. "Why not?"

Levi arched off the door. "Because it won't end well."

Something in his tone, something in the way Levi's voice shook around those words, made a warning sign flash in my mind, but when he nipped at my lower lip, I shoved it aside. He was here, so was I, and his mouth was so exquisite that I wanted to devour it.

I knew Levi thought I was a bad option, that I was going to break his heart. But the truth was that if there was one thing I was sure of, it was that I would never hurt this man. I would never break his heart because I'd rather rip mine out first.

"You need to trust me," I said, and slid my tongue along his lower lip. "Close your eyes, stop thinking, and just kiss me."

As his mouth parted, a low groan escaped me. I'd waited so long to have his lips back under mine, and now that I had him, there was no way I was about to let him go. Not without getting my fill of his sweet, sweet mouth.

I traced my fingers along his cheek and up his jaw, and then speared them in his hair. Levi slid his hand over my shoulder to tug me in close. I tangled my tongue with his, and when our chests met and a low moan rumbled out of him, I almost fell to my knees.

Fuck, that sound coming from him had my cock aching to get in on the action. But where I would usually be aiming for that, urging Levi to unlock the door, and let me come inside with him, I knew now what I had to do to win the trust I so desperately wanted from him.

Levi wanted me to prove he was more than just another notch in my bedpost. He wanted me to show him I wanted more from him.

Godfuckingdammit.

That meant going to bed tonight…alone.

Reluctantly, I pulled away, and as I released my hold of him, I brought my fingers up to touch my own lips, where his kiss lingered. "Delicious," I said. "Good night, Levi."

As I took a step back and Levi realized I was stopping, a frown marred his brow.

"Have sweet dreams," I told him, and flashed a smile. It was all I could do not to shove him up against the wall. Instead, I made myself head off toward my suite.

You can do it. One foot in front of the other.

"Killian?"

At the sound of Levi's voice, I glanced over my shoulder and knew if I didn't get out of there quick, this gentleman act I was trying to pull off would go right out the damn window.

"Yeah?"

"Everything okay?"

Other than me sacrificing what I want more than anything tonight to prove I'm in it for the long haul? "Yeah. I had a great time today."

"Okay." Levi shook his head and quickly schooled his features back to neutral. "Good night."

I gave a quick nod, and a second later he disappeared inside his room, and before I could change my mind and go to him, I ran to mine.

TWENTY

Killian

"WAIT, STOP. LET'S bring up the sound on Killian's mic and start again." Our tour director, Patrick, paced in front of the stage, glancing back to the mix booth in the rear of the stadium to make sure the sound engineers were following his orders.

When I got the thumbs-up from the crew, I spoke into the mic, and they continued to adjust the sound until Patrick shook his head.

"Can we get another mic?" he called out. "Anyone?"

"No one's coming to listen to Kill," Viper said, rolling his eyes. "Just turn it off."

I flipped him the finger as Levi called out from the wings, "I got it." He emerged onto the stage a few seconds later with a new mic.

It didn't escape my notice that he still wasn't looking my way, and hadn't other than a quick nod when we arrived at the venue. After finally thinking I'd gotten through to him during our day together, it was like he'd woken today with his walls back up.

Frustrating didn't even begin to cover it.

I took the mic off the stand, and when Levi reached for it, I held on tight until he looked at me.

When he finally glanced up, I smiled. "Hey."

"Hi." Damn. Clipped and businesslike as ever, nothing like the man I'd gone to dinner with last night. For fuck's sake. All that progress gone in one fell swoop.

He held the new mic out to me, and when I took it, he pulled the old one loose from my grip and walked back off the stage.

Seriously, what the fuck had I done? I'd been a perfect gentleman last night, when all I'd wanted to do was get him into his room and tear every perfectly starched piece of clothing off his body.

Levi was infuriating. Difficult. And more stubborn than anyone I'd ever met—and I worked with Viper, for Christ's sake.

Levi was apparently keen on making me work for it.

Focusing back on the soundcheck, I caught Viper smirking at me from across the stage, and it made me want to go over there and knock the expression right off his face. Smug bastard had already caught his guy, and he'd made it look easy.

Unfortunately for me, nothing about Levi Walker was easy.

I tested out the mic with a few words, the volume seemingly stronger now, and then Slade kicked off "Hard" again. I joined in, plucking the bass's strings so effortlessly that I didn't have to think about it anymore. We'd played this song and the others on our *Corruption* album so many times now that I could play them in my sleep if I had to. The thrill from the crowd hearing them never got old, but I was starting to feel anxious to write again, to make something new. Most of the songs on this album had been written by Halo and Viper, and while I loved them, I missed having my stamp on our stuff as well. Once we got back to New York, I'd be heading straight to the studio.

As the song ended, Patrick nodded at me. "Sounds good. Feel all right to you?"

"No problems," I said.

"Anyone else having an issue?"

"I heard Slade's having a hard time keeping it up," Jagger cracked.

Slade stood up behind his kit and aimed a drumstick at Jagger's head. "The fuck, man?"

"Not my fault. Just tryin' to help you out." Slade hurled the drumstick at Jagger, and as Jagger ducked the assault, he laughed. "Oh, did I say keeping it up? I mean keeping up. My bad."

As Slade moved out from behind the drums, an argument ensuing, I pulled my strap over my head and set the bass on the stand behind me for the crew to take care of. I wasn't about to stick around for one of Jagger and Slade's bromance throw-downs, no matter how entertaining they could be.

I had an obstinate band manager to deal with.

Levi wasn't in the wings when I ventured offstage, and when I asked some of the crew if they'd seen where he went, they all shrugged, like it wasn't their job to keep track of him.

Well, no, it wasn't, but that didn't help me any, did it?

When I did a full walk-through and still didn't catch a glimpse of him, I sighed and headed back to the dressing room to see if the food had been laid out yet.

As I pushed through the door, my feet came to a stop as the familiar blond head of hair I'd been searching for came into view.

Levi had a clipboard in his arms, and he seemed to be counting each can of soda, each bottle of water, and checking that all the food on our rider was accounted for.

"Figures I would find you here," I said, kicking the door shut behind me and turning the lock. Levi jerked his head in my direction and then looked to the locked door.

"I didn't realize you were looking for me."

Bullshit. Even with his polished manager facade back on, I could see the hint of what looked like guilt in his eyes.

"I was. I am." I crossed the room, stopping when I stepped into his personal space. Close enough to touch, but I kept my hands to myself.

For now.

Levi looked back down at the clipboard, making a note, affecting a bored tone as he said, "What can I do for you, Killian?"

Seriously? All that fucking buildup last night to start back at square one?

Forcing my voice to stay calm, as nonchalant as he seemed to be, I said, "I just wanted to see what's up."

With his gaze still averted, Levi shrugged. "Just checking on things. You?"

"Oh, you know, the same. Just…checking on *things*."

"Mhmm," he said absently, and as he continued to check off his list, ignoring me, I began to quickly lose my usually large reserve of patience. I snatched the pen out of Levi's hand and tossed it across the room, causing him to look up in surprise.

There. Finally.

Before he could say a word, I moved in behind him so that his front pressed up against the table. "There a problem, Levi?"

TWENTY-ONE

Levi

WITH MY HANDS braced on the table and the length of Killian's body aligned to mine, every one of my muscles tensed. I could feel his breath on my neck, and I shivered, a natural response for anyone so close to Killian Michaels in a *locked* room.

Exactly where I wanted him last night.

But he'd backed off for some reason, had given me a kiss that blew my head clean off my shoulders, and then left me in the doorway of my hotel room as hard and frustrated as I'd ever been in my life.

Yeah, that was the word for what I was feeling today —*frustrated.*

As Killian's hips pressed harder against my ass, I licked my suddenly dry lips, already forgetting his question. When I didn't respond, a humorless laugh left his throat, the vibrations rocking my body.

"I'm only going to ask one more time. Do we have a problem here, Levi?" Killian's voice was silky smooth, but there was an underlying edge to it that told me he wasn't in the mood for bullshit.

Good thing, because neither was I.

"Yeah," I said. "We might have a problem."

He must've been caught off guard by my answer, because he backed off me just enough that I had room to turn around and face him.

"I never thought you'd be a tease," I said, watching the frown he wore morph into a look of surprise.

"Excuse me?"

"You heard me." I took a step forward, causing Killian to back up until there was enough space between us that I wasn't at risk of grabbing him and doing something stupid like kissing him. "You spent hours yesterday trying to convince me we should try whatever this is only to blow me off? You told me this wasn't a game, and yet here we are."

"Whoa, whoa, whoa." Killian put his hands up. "You think I blew you off?"

I snorted. "Not literally, that's for sure."

"Wait...what?" Rubbing his forehead, he turned away only to spin back around. "You're pissed because I *didn't* invite myself inside last night?"

"Pretty sure you knew you had an open invitation." When Killian's face paled, I rolled my eyes. "Don't act so surprised. I was practically begging for it."

"Huh. Well, it would've been nice if you had actually *asked* for it instead of assuming."

"Doesn't matter now." Shrugging, I started back to the catering table to finish checking inventory, but Killian grabbed my arm.

"I was *trying* to be a nice guy. I was *trying* to give you what I thought you wanted."

"Guess there's a lot you still have to learn about me."

His hold on my arm stayed firm. "Does that mean I'll actually get the chance to?"

There it was, the dilated pupils and lust that glazed over his bright blue eyes when he looked at me. It was like striking a match—we both reached for each other at the same time, our lips crashing together, him grasping at my tie as I threaded my fingers through his dark hair, bringing him in closer.

Killian's mouth fit against mine perfectly, and when I ran my tongue along his lower lip, begging for entry, he gave it without hesitation. Hot, desperate breaths were all I could hear as we devoured each other, making up for lost time. He pulled me in closer, and there was no denying that whatever game he'd been teasing me with last night was over. He was hard behind his jeans, and as he gripped my ass to pull me even closer, my own erection strained with the need to be satisfied by this man, somehow, someway, right *now*.

I walked us forward until Killian's back hit the wall, and then I rubbed my covered dick alongside his, dying for some kind of relief even as his kiss left me dizzy and breathless. My rules flew out the window, the ones that said fooling around with clients was forbidden, as well as no fucking in the workplace.

Because that was what was about to happen here. What I wanted.

A good, long fucking. And I wanted it with the man making the hottest sounds of pleasure I'd ever heard.

"Still think this is a game?" Killian said, his breath hitching as he deftly unbuttoned my jeans. I pushed my hips forward, wanting his hands on me, needing—

A loud banging on the door made my thoughts shut down, both of us freezing as familiar voices shouted through the door.

"Hello?" Slade called out. More banging. "Why's the door fucking locked?"

"Let me try." The handle jiggled, and then Jagger pounded. "Yo, who's in there? Killian? You better not be eating all my chocolate koalas, man."

"Jesus Christ." Killian still gripped my open pants and both of us were breathing heavily, but as the pounding started again and one of the guys called for security to open the door, we both dropped our holds on each other.

My eyes were still on Killian's as I backed away, tucking in my shirt and buttoning it back up. His lips were red, his hair tousled from my hands being in it, and fuck, he'd never been sexier.

I want him, I thought. *I want him no matter the consequences.* I would've taken every piece of him if we hadn't been interrupted. I would've worshipped the rock god standing before me while on my knees, until my name was a prayer he uttered over and over again.

As Killian kicked off the wall, the voices outside grew louder. Reaching into my back pocket for my wallet, I quickly pulled out what I needed and held it out to Killian.

When he saw what it was, he grinned cockily.

"Room ten thirteen, in case you forgot," I said, as he took my spare room key and slid it into his pocket.

"Breaking the rules... I approve." Killian brushed his thumb across my lips.

Keys jingled outside the door, and I grabbed hold of his wrist.

"After the show," I said, nipping at the tip of his thumb. "Maybe we can break some more rules."

TWENTY-TWO

Killian

I WASN'T ONE to ever want a gig over and done, but Christ it felt like the night had been never-fucking-ending. How was I supposed to concentrate on the show with Levi's room key burning a hole in my back pocket? Not to mention he didn't watch from the wings like he usually did. Did that mean he was already back at the hotel waiting for me?

Yeah, with thoughts like that running through my mind, it was a good thing my hands had muscle memory, or I'd have fucked up the show in a big way.

Once we were backstage, I didn't waste any time. I grabbed my shit from the dressing room in seconds, but before I could head out to the car I had waiting out back, I heard Slade call out, "Yo, Kill, you comin' out with us?"

I shook my head, my hand on the door. "I've got plans."

"Plans without us?" Jagger said. "Rude."

No, rude would be leaving Levi waiting. 'Cause then he'd think too much, maybe overthink, and all that thinking could lead to changing his mind, and *that* was not fucking happening.

"Later," I said as I headed out the door, practically running to the idling SUV I'd reserved before going onstage. Less than ten minutes later I was in my hotel room, and ten minutes after that I was showered, dressed, and shoving a handful of condoms into my pocket—because after months, only one round with Levi wasn't going to satiate my hunger.

My heart was already pumping like I'd run a mile, and as I gave myself a once-over in the mirror, I flicked open another button on the shirt I didn't plan on wearing for long, and then smoothed a hand over my still-wet hair. I hadn't bothered shaving, so hopefully Levi had a thing for stubble.

I forced in a deep breath, holding it until my chest burned before letting it out.

Showtime.

With the key card Levi gave me in my hand, I made my way down the hall to his room. I didn't bother to knock, but tapped the card against the lock, and then I opened the door to darkness.

Quietly, I passed through the suite, stopping only when a sliver of light caught my attention.

Levi stood inside the bedroom by the window, his back to me as he looked out over the harbor, the Sydney Opera House lit up in the background. He wasn't wearing a shirt, and even from across the room I could make out the lean muscles of his back that led down to a pair of sweatpants hanging low around his hips.

Fuuuck.

As if he heard my thoughts, Levi turned around, resting his hands on the window seat as he looked my way. If I'd worried there'd be hesitation on his part, I didn't need to anymore; the look on his face told me everything I needed to know.

Serious as ever and ready to sin.

Licking my lips, I tossed the key card aside and sauntered into the room, Levi's eyes drinking me in. It was intense, that dark stare, almost as intense as the anticipation I could feel practically vibrating in the air between us. My heart continued to hammer as I drew closer, and then Levi pushed up off the seat.

I'd always wondered what he was hiding under those proper button-ups he wore, but the reality of Levi's naked skin as he stopped in front of me, close enough to touch, had my mouth watering.

He was long and lean, his olive skin smooth, with just a trail of hair leading down the strong V of his hips before disappearing under those sweatpants I wanted to rip off with my teeth.

Before I could drop to my knees to do just that, Levi grabbed the waistband of my jeans and tugged me closer, so close that I could taste his breath on my lips.

"So," he said, his voice low and husky. "How was the show?"

Teasing, drawing out the inevitable, that's what Levi was doing, but I wasn't in the mood to waste any more time. "What fuckin' show?" I said, before crashing my lips down on his.

His mouth met mine eagerly; he clearly didn't give a shit about his question as he pulled at my shirt. I shouldn't have bothered putting it on in the first place, and as Levi began to work his way up, unbuttoning the linen, my impatience took over.

Without taking my lips away from his, I ripped the damn thing off, buttons flying everywhere as I shrugged out of the shirt and threw it on the ground.

Levi let out a low chuckle and pulled his mouth free just enough so he could look at me. "Feeling needy, Killian?" He placed his hands on my shoulders and slowly ran them down my chest, leaving goosebumps in their wake.

God, I was already full-mast and raring to go from just looking at him, and when he dipped his fingers below the waist of my jeans, I couldn't help but moan. It was like everything was happening in slow motion, the torture of not having his mouth or hands on my cock or being inside him almost too much to take.

Another throaty chuckle left him, and then, as if he was making it his mission to drive me out of my goddamn mind, his lips grazed the sensitive skin along my neck, and I couldn't stop the shiver that went through me. My dick throbbed to the point of pain as Levi bit down on my lobe, and then he whispered, "I'll take that as a yes."

I nearly blacked out as Levi firmly wrapped his hand around my erection and gave a rough stroke.

Jesus Christ, I wasn't gonna make it. It'd been too long, and I'd wanted this too much, and…fuuuck.

My chest heaved with the exertion it took not to come as I grabbed Levi's arm hard. "Wait." I panted, waiting for the urge to pass. "Just…wait a second."

Confusion crossed Levi's face, and then, like he'd come to the wrong conclusion, he narrowed his eyes. "I swear to God, if you walk out of my suite after all this, I will—"

I shut him up with a kiss, still gripping his arm as I walked him back toward the bed. When I ripped my mouth free, I removed his hold and gave him a wicked grin.

"Don't think you're getting off that easy, Levi. I don't plan on leaving until both of us are thoroughly fucked." And then, before he could react, I shoved him down onto the bed.

TWENTY-THREE

Levi

SHIT.

AS MY ass hit the mattress, I reached out behind me to steady myself as I stared up at what could only be described as the best damn view I'd seen in my life.

Killian had stepped forward between my splayed thighs, and as I took in the picture he made, I couldn't stop myself from reaching for my hard-on. With his hair still damp from the shower he must've taken before arriving, a couple of strands fell forward into his eyes, which roamed over every inch of me he could see. His built chest continued to heave as his gaze dropped to my hand, and when he licked his swollen lips, still slick from mine, I pumped my hips up and gave myself a harder stroke.

"Fuckin' hell, Levi..."

He reached down to slowly unbutton his jeans, and my own impatience grew. I watched with greedy eyes, wanting more than anything to see the Killian from my fantasies standing naked in front of me, where I could finally touch him, finally have him touch me. And as if he knew just how much I wanted it, the sexy bastard paused at the button and brought his eyes to mine.

"Hmm, I like that sound."

Sound? What fucking sound?

"That groan you just made in the back of your throat," Killian said, and then slowly began to draw the zipper down. "That didn't sound frustrated, that sounded— What did you call me?"

How he expected me to think as he reached inside his jeans and freed his cock was beyond me. But when it finally appeared, and I got my first look of what I wanted inside me as soon as possible, I licked my lips, and Killian chuckled.

"Ah, yes, *needy*."

My hand automatically squeezed my cock at the sound of Killian's raspy voice, and then he chuckled.

"Lie back on the bed, Levi."

Not about to argue, I scooted back on the plush white duvet, my hands and body sinking into the material that reminded me of a cloud. With my eyes locked on Killian, I paused when I reached the middle of the bed, and before I lay back, I reached for the elastic band of my sweats, more than ready to get them the hell out of the way.

"Uh ah," Killian said as he placed a knee on the mattress, and then—*holy shit*—crawled his way up my body. "Getting you naked is my job tonight." When he reached my cotton-covered erection and stopped, I swallowed and craned my head to look down at him just to be sure I wasn't imagining this.

But no, I could feel Killian's warm breath through my pants, teasing my dick, and when he slipped his fingers into the waistband and began to tug them off, I automatically raised my hips, wanting to be naked with him, wanting it all.

"You don't know how long I've wanted this," Killian said so softly, so reverently that it almost sounded as though he was talking to himself. But when he raised his head and his smoldering eyes found mine, it was clear his message was for me, and me alone.

The smile that crossed his lips was downright immoral. He tugged my sweats all the way off and then tossed them off the end of the bed, then moved to his knees and subjected me to the most scorching once-over I'd ever received.

"You are the best fucking thing I've ever seen in my life," he said, as he shoved his hand into his jeans and fisted his length, and there was no way I wasn't about to reciprocate. I wrapped my fingers around my aching shaft, and as I bent my legs and placed my feet on the duvet, a loud growl left Killian's throat.

"Yes. Fuck, yes," he said, as his eyes dropped to my hand, and his moved in time with mine. "Show me how fucking hot you are for me...for us."

My heart pounded in time to my pulsing dick, and as I trailed my gaze up from Killian's busy hand to his rippling abs with all their dips and angles, I suddenly wanted him closer. I wanted him over me, under me, close enough that I could run my hands and tongue all over him. "Come down here."

Killian licked his lips and then got to his feet to shove his jeans free. When he kicked them aside and moved back to the bed, my hips thrust up from the mattress again. God, he was beautiful, and as he made his way back up the bed toward me, my cock throbbed to the point of aching.

Killian Michaels naked was one visual I would never want to get out of my head. He was perfection. Every rippling muscle, every hair on his head and sprinkled over his body. He was a work of art, and as he settled down over the top of me and his legs moved between mine, I wrapped my arms around his neck and arched up into him, finally getting the contact I'd been so desperately craving.

Killian shuddered over me, then he lowered his head and whispered against my mouth, "If you keep doing that, I'm going to come on you instead of in you."

I groaned, already imagining how damn good it was going to feel stretched and filled by his cock, and then nipped at Killian's lower lip.

"Hmm, now that would be a shame. I can't tell you how many times I've gotten off to"—I kissed my way up Killian's jaw to his ear—"the thought of you coming on me."

"Fuuuck," Killian said, as I wrapped my legs around his waist and, with a quick shove, rolled him to his back and straddled his waist.

I smoothed my palms up over his chest until I planted them by his head on the pillow, and then I leaned down to press a hard kiss to his lips. "Mmm, you're right. Let's do that instead."

TWENTY-FOUR

Killian

HOT FUCKING DAMN. I'd known Levi would be worth the wait, but as I looked up at him from where I was lying flat on his bed, I realized just how much I'd underestimated my feelings for him.

Lean, confident, and just as bossy in bed as he was out of it, Levi was everything I'd fantasized about and more. His tight thigh muscles flexed, and he pushed up to fully straddle my waist.

With the bed cloaked in shadows, except for the sliver of city lights from outside, I could barely make out Levi's features, and as far as I was concerned, that just wouldn't do.

I wanted the full experience tonight.

I wanted to touch Levi. I wanted to taste him. And more than anything else in the world, I wanted to see his expression when I slid inside him for the first time and made him mine.

"Levi?" I said, smoothing my hands up the sides of his thighs. "The light? Turn it on. I want to see you."

Levi leaned off to the side to flick on a lamp, and as the soft glow filled the room and he moved back to sit over my thighs, I zeroed in on his lithe frame. Jesus, he was stunning, a goddamn masterpiece, and as I ran my gaze over every naked inch of him, a growl rumbled out of my throat and I dug my fingers into his thighs.

"Fucking gorgeous," I said, as Levi stared down at me, dark eyes dilated, his lust and arousal right there for me to see. "*You* are fucking gorgeous."

Levi slicked his tongue over his lower lip and then reached for his delicious dick. He slowly began to stroke himself as a blissed-out moan fell from his lips.

My cock throbbed as Levi began to roll his hips forward. My eyes locked on the show he was putting on for me, as he pushed his leaking dick through his fist over and over again.

He moaned softly on every stroke, as his eyes trailed a fiery path all over me. He worked his length as well as I played my guitar, and when I was no longer able to lie still under such temptation, I jacked my hips up in response to his sensual stroking.

A wickedly hot smirk tipped up one corner of Levi's mouth, then he reached for my erection with his free hand. The feel of his fingers wrapping around my overly sensitized skin made my eyes slam shut.

"Mmm." Levi's throaty hum made my eyes reopen, and when I saw him looking down at my cock as he squeezed and stroked—as though measuring me to see what was about to get all up in him—my balls tingled with anticipation. "I want this."

Christ. I'd waited so damn long for this, wanted him so damn much. To actually hear Levi admit to wanting me was almost enough for me to die a happy man—*almost.*

"Then why don't you come up here and take it?"

The look he aimed my way was incendiary. "Because I'm taking a moment to enjoy you." Levi gave another hard pull of my length and then swiped his thumb over the plump head, making me curse. "It's not every day I have a sexy rock star in my bed."

"Levi…" I said between clenched teeth, my control vanishing under his teasing words and torturous touch.

"Killian," he said, his voice a breathy sigh as he released us and moaned.

"Get down here—*now*."

The second he was close enough to grab, I put one of my hands behind his neck and the other on his cheek, and then Levi's mouth was on mine. As his cock grazed up against my erection, I punched my hips up, and a soft grunt left him and entered my mouth. He then found the pillow under my head, and as he gripped it and began to really move over the top of me, I trailed my fingers from his neck down to his back, and then grabbed a handful of his tight ass.

As I pulled Levi's body flush to mine, he groaned gutturally and shuddered over the top of me. I shoved my tongue inside his mouth, and as Levi began to suck on it, he rocked his hips back and forth as though my cock was already deep inside him.

He was hot as fuck, and not shy in the least about going after what he wanted. When Levi tore his mouth free and stared down at me, I knew I was done for.

Levi Walker was pure perfection, and nothing and nobody would ever be able to compare.

TWENTY-FIVE

Levi

MY ENTIRE BODY felt as though it were a live wire with how tightly strung I was. One of Killian's hands was cupping my face, and his other was gripping my ass. I was about as close to him as I could possibly be without being connected, and nothing could have prepared me for the intensity of this moment.

I'd known going into tonight that the likelihood of keeping some kind of barrier up when it came to my heart and this man would be difficult. But the emotions in Killian's eyes as he looked up at me demolished any walls that were in his way.

Damn he was sexy. His dark hair was a disheveled mess on the white pillow his head rested on. His lips were red and swollen. And the long, thick cock and body I was rubbing my dick all over was such a fucking turn-on that it was a miracle I hadn't come all over him the second he was under me.

Killian Michaels was under me. And as if that wasn't enough to make me hard, the knowledge that he was between *my* legs, and about to be inside *my* body, had me raring to go all night.

I let go of the pillow and stroked my thumb over his lips. Killian opened them and sucked it in.

"Shit, Levi." His groan was pained as I pulled my thumb free. "I need to get my fucking jeans."

I narrowed my eyes, and he grabbed my ass with both hands and craned up off the bed to nip at my lip. "Condom. Lube. They're in my jeans."

Ahh, okay. Got it. But luckily for him, I wasn't the kind of man to ever forget the finer details. Really, he should've known better.

With a hand on his shoulder, I shoved him back to the mattress, and when he started to protest, I shook my head. "Don't you know by now that I'd never come to such an important meeting unprepared?"

I leaned over him and reached under the opposite pillow, where I'd placed several condoms and a bottle of lube.

When Killian caught sight of my stash, he grinned at me. "Why'd you hide 'em, then? Worried I'd toss you on the bed the second I saw them?"

I picked up one of the condoms. "No, I was worried I'd toss you on it." I brought the packet to my lips and tore it open with my teeth.

"Always gotta be in control, huh? The boss in *and* out of the bedroom."

I tongued my top lip and rolled the condom down his throbbing length. "Would you really want me any other way?"

Killian snatched up the bottle of lube, uncapped it, and poured a good amount into his talented hands. "Don't *you* know by now, I want you anyfuckingway I can get you. So get down here, where I can get you good and ready for me."

Killian's words and demand made my dick jerk, and when I leaned over him and he began to slip and slide his fingers up and down my crack, I closed my eyes and burrowed my face into the crook of his neck. God, it'd been too damn long since

I'd felt this good, and as Killian massaged the tip of his finger over my entrance, I couldn't help the eager moan that left me.

"Oh yeah, I like that fucking sound." Killian probed a little more, and as his finger slipped past the tight ring of muscle, he said, "Let's see if I can make you make it again."

As his long digit slipped inside me, he got his wish. A deep, pleasure-filled moan left me, and I shoved back on him.

Killian turned his head on the pillow until we were eye to eye. "Music to my fucking ears," he said, as he slowly pulled his finger free, then pushed two inside.

I cursed and squeezed my eyes shut, clenching around what was invading my body, wanting to keep it exactly where it was. But Killian was relentless with his slow and steady finger fuck, sliding his fingers in and out until my toes curled and my body vibrated.

"Fuck, Killian..." I muttered, and then I rose over him on my knees. I needed more, and I needed it now, and as I looked down at his sex-flushed face, sinful smirk, and blistering-hot stare, the pleasure was almost more than I could bear.

Killian slowly withdrew his fingers and reached down to grip his cock to tease me with the wide head.

Then he threw my words from earlier back at me—"Yeah... let's do that"—and entered me with one solid thrust.

My shout was equal to Killian's. It was desperate and raw, the sound of two people caught up in a maelstrom of pleasure so extreme, so unreal, that it was physically impossible to keep quiet.

I stilled for a moment, adjusting to sitting astride Killian's lap, and as our eyes locked and he ran his hands up my thighs, I slowly began to move again. I rocked forward, thrilling at the impressive thickness now stretching me wide, and when Killian began driving up inside me, I licked my lips and reached for my dick.

"Oh fuck," Killian said, as I began to stroke, my mind shutting down to anything other than the exquisite way Killian's body was making me feel. "Levi... Jesus. You feel and look so damn good."

Letting go of my shaft, I placed my hands on Killian's tight abs, and as I ran them up his torso and over his ribs to his chest, he began to pump faster. Up and down, Killian drilled in and out of me, as my body moved over the top of his like a well-oiled machine.

I panted and dug my fingers into Killian's pecs every time he penetrated me, and when he moved his hands down to my ass to hold me still, I braced myself. He trembled beneath me, his cock pulsing inside me, as I lowered my head and took his mouth in a savage kiss.

I bit and sucked at his lips and shoved my tongue inside to taste him, and as his muscles tensed and his fingers flexed into my skin so hard I knew they'd bruise, I said, "I'm in so much damn trouble with you. Come in me, Killian. Give me what you've always wanted to."

Killian gave a final thrust of his hips, his dick rubbing against the exact spot I needed to make me see stars. As I moaned, hot jets of cum shot out, coating his phenomenal body, and that was all Killian needed to lose his control.

With his eyes shut, he craned his head back into the pillow and arched up, sinking him even deeper inside me. I nipped at his chin and kissed my way up his jaw, and not a second later, the sexiest sound I'd ever heard roared out of him, as he tensed and then began to tremble.

As the storm subsided, and he pulled me down until I was flush against him, I ran my fingers across his chest and basked in the delicious aftermath.

Finally. I'd finally had Killian inside me, and while he'd told me he knew *I'd* be worth the wait, I wondered how shocked he'd be to know that he'd been worth every argument, every moment of worry I'd ever had about being attracted to a client.

I hadn't been lying when I told him I was in trouble here
—I was.

Deep, deep trouble. Because after this, I knew I would give
up everything I had to make Killian mine. Including my dream
job, which had brought me into his life in the first place.

TWENTY-SIX

Levi

"SO," I SAID, my chest moving in time with his as we each tried to catch our breath after round three. "Still think I was worth it?"

Killian trailed his fingers down my spine but otherwise remained silent, and when I raised my head to look into his eyes, he grinned and lightly smacked my ass. "Totally fucking worth it. That was…"

When words failed him, I said, "I'll take your inability to think of a fitting adjective as a compliment."

Killian grabbed a handful of my ass and rolled us over until my back hit the mattress. Then he pulled out of me, rolled off the condom, and said, "I'm gonna go toss this and grab a washcloth and towel. But I promise you, by the time I come back, I'll have plenty of ways to describe just how amazing you, and *that*, was."

As Killian shoved up and hopped off the bed, I drank in the sight of his sweat-slicked body and licked my lips. I had no idea what time it was, how long we'd been sating the insatiable lust that roared between us. Something told me the sun would rise before my hunger abated.

"You didn't fall asleep on me, did you?" Killian asked, as he sauntered back into the room, a towel in hand and a self-satisfied smile on his mouth. "I mean, I know I've been working you overtime and all, but I'm not nearly done with you yet."

"And here I thought I was off the clock."

"As a rock band's manager, you should know by now you're never off the clock."

As Killian climbed back on the bed, he tossed me the towel and stretched out beside me. "So what would you call this?" I asked.

Killian ran his eyes down me. "A one-on-one personal client consultation."

I scoffed. "And *what* exactly are we consulting on?"

"Compatibility?"

"Hmm," I said, and tossed the towel aside now that I was done with it. "I can see how that's important."

"Very," Killian agreed, stroking his fingers along my hip. "I mean, I don't let just anyone see me so naked and…vulnerable."

My eyes dropped to Killian's stiffening length, and I arched an eyebrow. "You don't look too vulnerable to me."

"It's a nervous condition."

"And I make you nervous?"

Killian reached for my hand and drew it up to his chest. "The way you make me feel makes me nervous."

My heart thumped as I stared into Killian's blue eyes. What I saw there made me want to dive headfirst into everything and anything with him. "You really mean that, don't you?"

Killian leaned over and brushed his lips across mine. "Finally, you're listening."

"Well, your cock *is* pretty persuasive."

His mouth fell open and his eyes widened.

"What?"

"I was trying to be sincere," Killian said.

"I know. So was I."

Killian chuckled. "You know, I think I like this side of you."

"You *think*? I thought you were sure," I teased.

Rolling his eyes, he said, "If I say something sincere here, are you going to make fun of me?"

"I'll think twice about it." When Killian groaned, I laughed and pushed against his chest. "I'm kidding. I just never knew you could be so…sweet."

"Keep it up and I won't be."

"Okay, okay. What were you gonna say? No smartass retort here, promise."

When he shook his head, I crossed my heart. He sighed.

"You asked me if I was sure about this. Levi, I was sure about you from the minute you walked into my life."

"See, when you say things like that, it makes me want to believe you."

"Then why don't you?"

I swallowed hard. "I think I'm starting to."

"Good. Because you have to know I would never hurt you."

I wanted so badly to trust what Killian was telling me, I really did. But I wasn't one to let myself easily fall. Not after the pain of what I'd gone through the last time.

But maybe…just maybe…this time would be different.

"Let me in," Killian said, leaning his forehead against mine. "Let me be the one for you."

As I lay there in Killian's arms, the night settling in around us, I found myself drifting off and imagined what it would be like to belong to Killian, and for him to belong to me.

TWENTY-SEVEN

Killian

_____

BAM BAM BAM.

The sound of someone pummeling the door startled me out of a deep sleep as someone shot up from the bed beside me.

Not just someone—Levi.

Holy shit. I was still in his room. I barely remembered passing out, though it couldn't have been that long ago.

Pushing up on my elbow, I rubbed the back of my hand over my eyes and watched as Levi picked up the sweatpants he'd been wearing last night. The sun filtered in through the curtains, lighting him up, his luscious backside on full display.

Beneath the sheet resting at my hips, my cock jerked, more than ready for another round.

BAM BAM BAM. "Why is no one answering their fucking door?" Viper yelled.

Levi froze and looked back at me. He didn't need to say anything; in two seconds flat I was up, wrapping the sheet around my waist as I moved out of sight.

What the hell did Viper want so early?

Before the banging could start again, I could hear Levi unlocking the door and pulling it open. Keeping my back against the wall, I scooted closer to the edge, still staying out of sight, so I could hear what was being said.

Viper let out a low whistle. "Didn't realize you worked out, Levi."

Shit, he didn't bother with a shirt, did he? Not that I could blame him—he should be naked all day, every day—but I didn't need Viper getting an eyeful of what was mine.

Mine…? When did I start thinking of Levi as mine?

Levi cleared his throat. "What do you need, Viper?"

"What I *need* is for you assholes to answer your goddamn doors." *Such a temperamental little shit.*

"Mine's open, so what's the problem?"

"Killian isn't answering his."

There was a pause, and then Levi said, "And that would be my problem because…?"

"Because Kill always answers his fucking door. And his phone. He's not answering that either."

Oh shit, my phone. I didn't even know where it was… maybe still in my jeans pocket? Hell, I didn't know where those were either.

Viper let out an exaggerated sigh. "I tried Slade's room, Jagger's room, fucking Imogen's room…no one is answering for shit."

"While I appreciate being a last resort, maybe you can tell me what this emergency is."

I could hear what sounded like paper shifting. "I came up with an idea for a song, and I need Kill's input on something."

"And?" Levi said.

"And what? I just told you."

"So you're telling me you're banging down everyone's doors because you need Killian's input on a song?"

"Glad you're paying attention," Viper said, ever the smartass. I half hoped Levi would either punch him or shut the door in his face.

Levi muttered something, which wasn't nearly as satisfying as Viper getting the smackdown he deserved. I wasn't about to pop out there to do it and give myself away.

But maybe later.

"Viper, why don't you give him a break? I'm sure he'll call you when he's up, and you can work on it then."

"Coming from the man who hand-delivers our itineraries before the ass-crack of dawn. Wait…speaking of which, why do you look like you just woke up?"

"Couldn't sleep," Levi replied smoothly.

"Why not?"

"Believe it or not, Viper, being your manager requires putting out a lot of fires."

"Fires? What fires? I haven't beaten down any paparazzi in months."

"Maybe you're not the problem this time."

"Or maybe you're full of shit." Even without looking at him, I could practically see the sneer on Viper's face. "So you're sure you haven't seen Killian anywhere? You know, before I go banging on more doors."

Levi let out an exasperated sigh. "No, but if I see him before you do, I'll make sure to tell him you're having a crisis."

"You do that." A few seconds passed, and then Viper said, "By the way…"

"Yes, Viper?"

"When you're trying to be a sneaky fucker, you really should make sure Killian's clothes aren't all over the floor first. You know. If you wanted it to be a *secret*."

Motherfucker.

A stunned silence followed, and then Viper burst into the room, laughing as he caught sight of me standing against the wall with half the bedsheet around my hips.

"Goddammit, Viper," I said, pushing off the wall as he grinned like the cat that ate the canary.

Viper held his hands up, amusement sparking his eyes. "Oh, please, don't let me interrupt. This is just too good. And...*inappropriate*. Wouldn't you say?"

"V," I started, but he cut me off.

"I was talking to Levi," he said, looking over at the man walking back into the room with annoyance written all over his face. "Picking favorites now, huh?"

"Give it a rest, Viper," Levi responded.

"Our bassist and our manager." Viper tsked, enjoying catching us way too much. "What will all the others think?"

"I think you're assuming you're gonna be able to talk once you leave this room," I said, walking forward with one hand still holding the sheet.

"Ooh, threats. While I'd love to see you make good on those, Kill, you're a lover, not a fighter."

When I lunged toward Viper, Levi held me back.

Viper laughed again as he patted Levi on the shoulder. "Glad to see you finally gave in. I was beginning to worry Kill had lost it."

This time Levi lunged forward, pushing Viper toward the door and then wrangling it open with one hand. Once he had Viper out in the hallway, he said something I couldn't hear, and then the door slammed shut.

Viper's chuckles grew fainter as he seemed to go back to wherever the hell he was heading, but he was no longer my concern.

Levi was.

TWENTY-EIGHT

Levi

THERE WAS NO doubt in my mind that what Viper had just seen would make its rounds among the rest of the band members and the crew in a matter of hours, if not minutes. His big mouth got him into trouble constantly, and even his close friendship with Killian wouldn't stop him from being a gossipy shit. That was the reason I hadn't bothered wasting my breath by asking him not to say anything.

Well, maybe that was a small part of the reason.

The biggest part was Killian, who was watching me with what looked like trepidation in his eyes.

He approached me slowly, one of his arms up like he was trying to tame a wild animal.

"Levi, I'm so sorry," he said, stopping before he reached me, not even within touching distance.

"Why? It's not your fault."

"I'll go talk to him. Tell him not to say anything—"

I reached for his wrist, slowly lowering his arm. "Don't worry about it."

"But—"

"But what? Do you honestly think talking to Viper will get him to change his mind? Shut the fuck up for once?"

Killian seemed to think that over. "Probably not."

"Exactly." I shrugged and dropped my hold on him. "So let's not worry about it."

"Let's not worry about it," he repeated, looking at me strangely. "Are you… I mean, you're okay with…this?"

I raised a brow. "This?"

"People knowing. About us."

Huh. Maybe I should've been worried. After all, part of my brain was screaming at me that what we were doing would only end in disaster, that I knew better than to play with fire. I'd shocked even myself when I handed over my room key, but I couldn't say I regretted it. Not one bit. Not after last night.

How the hell could I?

I took a step toward him, coming toe to toe, and ran my hand down his arm. "Are *you* okay with it?"

Beneath my fingers, Killian's skin broke out in goosebumps. It felt intoxicating, eliciting that reaction from such a strong, beautiful man. It still wasn't lost on me that he was here when he could choose to be anywhere.

But I'd chosen my bed, I'd lain in it, and it was too late for regrets. I had to trust that Killian wasn't just telling me what I wanted to hear, that he hadn't pursued me for one night or a short fling. I had to trust he was all in.

"I've made my intention toward you pretty damn clear, but in case you're having doubts, I'm more than okay with anyone and everyone knowing, as long as I can have you," Killian said, placing his hand along my jaw and running his thumb over my lower lip. "But I asked you first."

Damn if his words didn't have my heart skipping a beat. To be wanted by Killian would have anyone feeling like the king of the world.

But if this was going to happen between us, there had to be rules. When I said as much, he laughed.

"Of course. Rules, right. Give it to me, then."

"Number one, this can't interfere with our jobs. No matter what happens, it can't cause problems with the band or with the management team."

Killian nodded. "Agreed."

"Number two, there's no one else."

A smile slowly crossed Killian's face. "Done before you asked. Is that all?"

"No." I reached down to where the bedsheet still covered the lower half of his body and, with a quick tug, let it drop to the floor. "You're required to be at my sexual beck and call at all times. Late nights, weekends, full days off…"

"Mmm, I don't see a problem with that." Killian wrapped his arms around my waist and then slid his hands down beneath my sweatpants, grabbing hold of my ass and kneading. "But that goes both ways, you know. I'll be at your beck and call if you'll be at mine."

He brushed his lips against mine once, twice, and when I moaned out a "yes," he hauled me back toward the bed for round…

Damn. I'd already lost count.

TWENTY-NINE

Levi

"CAN WE GET a round of whiskey sours? Thanks," I said to the guy behind the hotel's bar as I slid onto one of the barstools, Liam doing the same beside me. I winced as I settled onto the hard padding, every one of my muscles protesting any kind of movement after the hours I'd spent with Killian last night and most of today.

It'd been more than worth it.

Liam glanced at me from beneath the bill of his ball cap. "Lookin' a little stiff there, bro."

"Feeling it," I said, reaching for my drink.

"Oh yeah? There a reason for that?" Before I could answer, he took a sip and shuddered. "Damn, that's sour."

"Hence the name."

"Ugh." He wiped the back of his hand over his mouth and then flagged down the bartender. "Can I get a whiskey and Coke?" When he had his replacement in hand, he pushed his whiskey sour my way. "Now tell me your news."

"How do you know I have news?"

"Seriously? Have you been gone so long you've forgotten how our mystical twin powers work?"

I snorted out a laugh. "Guess so."

"Okay, let me see if I can figure this out without you telling me." Closing his eyes, Liam massaged his temples and hummed. "I see a dark shadow hunting you... Wait, it's not a shadow. It's a guy. Wait, no... Oh shit. It's not a guy, it's a god. A rock god. And I keep hearing the word 'kill...'"

I shoved Liam's shoulder, practically knocking him off the stool, and he laughed.

"Lucky guess," I said.

"Nah." Liam hopped back onto the seat and swallowed down some of his drink. "Anyone with eyes can see what's going on."

"What? Seriously?"

"Uh, yeah. That a problem?"

"No," I said automatically. "Yes. Hell, I don't know."

"Huh. Well, maybe it's just me that sees, then." Liam raised his eyebrows twice in quick succession. "So you gonna give me all the dirty details, or do I have to beg?"

"You? Beg. Yeah, right." I took a long sip and then rolled the glass on the bar between my hands. "I broke all my rules last night."

The corner of Liam's mouth twitched. "The ones that say fucking is off the table?"

"The ones that say fucking around with a *client* is off the table. Yes."

"You telling me you spent the night with Killian Michaels?"

The bartender froze as he came to a stop in front of us, surprise on his face as he glanced between me and Liam.

"He's joking," I said, so the bartender wouldn't go run to the nearest phone to call every friend and acquaintance he ever met. It must've worked, because he gave an uneasy smile and then slowly backed away.

When he was out of earshot, I smacked the shit out of Levi's arm. "Would you keep your voice down?"

"You're the one that wanted to have this conversation at a public bar."

I rubbed my forehead and groaned. "This was a mistake."

"Nah, we'll just use a different name. Like a code name."

I squinted at my brother. "A code name?"

"Yeah, you know, like Maverick or some shit."

"Maverick? Jesus…"

"No, Maverick works better in this case, though Jesus is probably easier to remember when you're screaming 'oh God' all night." Liam, the damn instigator, winked, and I surprised myself by not getting up and walking out of there. But I told my brother everything, and while he always gave me a hard time, he was always teasing. I knew I had his full support no matter what I did, and along with that, his brutal honesty. It was the latter I was here for.

"Okay, so you and *Maverick*," Liam said. "You had a good time with this Maverick fellow?"

"You're ridiculous, you know that, right?" I could only shake my head as I prepared to spill my guts. "Yeah, I had a good time. A great time. The best time of my fucking life."

Liam whistled. "Maverick's got skills, huh?"

I tried to bite back the smile that wanted to come out, but it was a struggle that ultimately failed. "You have no idea."

"Well, I *could* have an idea, seeing as he wanted to use those skills on me first—"

I shoved him clear off the barstool this time, smirking as he fell on his ass.

"Dude, I was joking," he protested, clambering back to his feet. "Try that shit again, and you're goin' down with me."

"Talk about Kil—uh, Maverick again and you won't be able to get back up."

"Touché." He chuckled, wiping off the back of his jeans. When he settled back beside me, he finished off his drink and raised his hand for another. This time, he waited for the drink to arrive before starting back up again. "So you like this guy enough to break your rules."

"Apparently so." I reached for a napkin and wiped the condensation off the sides of the glass. "I didn't want to. I tried not to give in, honest to God I did, but..."

"But?"

"Guess my self-control wasn't as strong as I thought."

"Bullshit. You've been around temptation for years and you never gave in, not since Jon—" Liam stopped himself and shook his head. "What I mean to say is, if you didn't think this Maverick was worth breaking your rules for, you wouldn't have done it."

"Simple as that, huh?"

"Simple as that," Liam agreed, then paused to take another sip of his drink. "Is that what you needed? Confirmation you did the right thing?"

I set my now-empty glass down and rubbed my hands on my pants. "I guess I asked you here to tell me I didn't completely fuck myself because of it."

"Do you regret it?"

"No," I said quickly.

"Then there's your answer."

"No, I... I mean, of course I don't regret it. He's amazing, Kil—Maverick," I said, catching myself as I noticed the bartender coming closer out of the corner of my eye. "Perfect, really. He's just a good guy. You know? He's nothing like so many of the groups I've worked with, all that drugs and groupies and rock 'n' roll shit. Well, I'm sure there were groupies—I mean, look at him—but not since I started managing the band, which in rock years is...forever." I fiddled with a stray string at the seam of my pants and made a note to have them tailored. "He's funny and charming and...sweet."

When Liam's eyebrows shot up, I laughed.

"He is sweet. Don't go telling anyone that, for God's sake. He does have a rep to uphold."

"Hmm." Liam stroked the scruff on his jaw. "I think you've fallen for this guy. I think it's a completely foreign concept to you and now you're doubting yourself because of it, but if you want my advice—"

"I do."

"Stop fighting so hard, bro. You take it all so seriously: your job, your love life—well, when you have one. You were the one who told me we don't need anyone's permission to go after what we want. So take your own advice. You're not gonna fuck this up."

When he clamped his hand down on my shoulder, I looked at him and nodded. "Thanks, Li. I needed to hear that."

"Anytime." He lifted his glass to his lips and frowned when he realized it was empty. That frown deepened when he looked up and down the bar, finding it empty as well. "Where the hell did he go?"

Shrugging, I said, "I'll be right back. Grab me another whiskey sour, would ya?" I stood up, and as I went to leave, I ran smack into the missing bartender. Or, rather, I ran straight into the tray of shots he'd been carrying.

I cursed, staring down at the liquor streaking my shirt and pants as Liam burst into laughter behind me.

"Graceful, bro. Hey, maybe *Maverick* will wanna lick it all off?"

I shot him a glare over my shoulder, but what he'd said wasn't a bad idea.

Great. Now all I was going to think about all night was Killian running his tongue all over my body.

Suddenly, I couldn't wait to get upstairs.

THIRTY

Killian

Fallin', fallin', fallin' for you
From the second I saw you it was all I could do
To keep my distance and try to forget you
But I'm fallin', fallin', fallin' for you...

I tapped my pencil against my chin as I stared at the notepad in front of me. For the last two hours I'd been playing around with a tune I couldn't get out of my head. It was a slow melody that reminded me of a heartbeat, and it wasn't lost on me why I suddenly had a desire to sit down and write again—*Levi*.

The idea had come to me earlier this morning when we'd been stretched out in his bed, Levi curled up into my side, his cheek naturally resting against my chest and his fingers trailing patterns all over my skin.

God. I was in so deep with him. So fucking deep that the second I'd left his suite and entered mine, I had automatically gone for my notepad and guitar. Emotions, whether good or bad, were always the catalyst when it came to my music and writing. Nothing was more inspiring than hating someone, or in my case love—

Yeah, "deep" might be a bit of an understatement. But I wasn't stupid. I knew what I felt, and considering I had never come close before, it didn't take a genius to know why I'd sworn off every single person alive the second Levi entered my life.

But it was way too early in this relationship to go there. Fuck, I'd only just managed to convince him to go on a date, kiss me…sleep with me. God forbid I slip up and actually say that out loud to Levi. The guy would run for the fucking hills. I needed to slow my roll, think of this as the beginning, something casual—something exclusive, but casual. That seemed more to Levi's liking, right? Right.

Tossing my pencil on the notepad, I took the pick from between my lips and began to strum again. As my fingers found the chords I was looking for, I began to hum along as the melody became more familiar. Then I closed my eyes and added the lyrics, the song a sexy ballad that would make hearts melt all around the world, the second Halo added his angelic voice to it.

Just as I was getting into the rhythm of it, a brisk knock on my door interrupted my train of thought, and I groaned and glared at the offending noise. Getting to my feet, I didn't bother putting my guitar down. I walked across the suite, my goal to see who was on the other side and send them on their way. Then I'd get right back to creating.

With my guitar in one hand, I reached for the handle with the other, and when I pulled the door open I found the one person I had no problem stopping for. Hell, the one person I had no problem doing anyfuckingthing for.

But something wasn't right. Levi was supposed to be hanging out with his brother for the next few hours. I'd reluctantly let him go when he told me it was kind of rude to fly Liam all the way out to another country and then ignore him.

But there was something else wrong with this picture, beyond the fact that Levi was at my door instead of downstairs at the bar, and that would be the way his bright yellow button-up was clinging to his gorgeous chest—not that I was complaining.

"Well, hi there," I said, holding the door open as I ran my eyes up and down the stunning man opposite me.

Levi's eyes dropped to the acoustic in my left hand and then came back to mine. "Hi. I'm sorry, did I interrupt you?"

"Yes," I said, and when Levi backed up a step, I chuckled. "Ask me if I care."

Levi eyed me, and when he didn't bother asking, already knowing the answer, I stepped aside.

Levi didn't hesitate, but as he walked past and I shut the door behind him, I asked, "Is it wet night t-shirt down at the bar? Not that I'm complaining. But next time, can you let me know? I'd like to be there when you decide to pour whatever it is all over yourself."

Levi glanced over his shoulder at me, and the smoldering look in his eyes was so damn hot that I was surprised I didn't melt to the floor.

"Not wet t-shirt night, no."

"So what's all over your shirt?"

As I walked around him and laid the guitar down on the couch, Levi came up beside me and said, "Why don't you put your mouth on me, and see if you can guess."

My cock stiffened as though he'd just sucked it, and judging by the sinful gleam in his eyes, he knew it. "Come 'ere."

Levi took a step closer, and I wound an arm around his waist, bringing that phenomenal body right back where it belonged—against mine. I could feel his erection against my thigh and smoothed my hand down over his perfectly fitted pants to grab his ass and tug him even closer. Then I brought my other hand up and ran my thumb over the open collar of his shirt.

Levi's eyes dropped to my lips, and as I sucked my thumb, he moaned.

Sweet. Levi's skin currently tasted as sweet as his mouth, and when I pulled my thumb free I said, "You taste like a chocolate cake."

Levi angled his chin up, giving me better access, then licked his lips. "And do you *like* chocolate cake?"

I kissed my way along his jaw, down his neck, where I tongued the base of his throat, then I bit and sucked my way back up to his ear and said, "I could eat chocolate cake all fucking night."

"Shit," Levi said, and rocked his hips against mine, looking for more friction. I shoved my leg between his thighs and hauled him up on it. Levi wrapped his arms around my neck and said, "I need a shower. I'm a mess…"

"Mmm…a delicious mess."

"Killian—"

"A shower, huh?" I said as I loosened my grip on his tight ass. "I think I have one of those."

"Oh yeah?"

"Yeah. But to use it, there's payment."

Levi grinned as I took his hand, leading him toward the en suite. "Oh I can't wait to hear what that is."

I threw a smile his way. "Come with me, and you'll find out."

THIRTY-ONE

Levi

WITH MY HAND in Killian's, I followed him into the en suite, and once we were inside, he shut and locked the door behind us.

"I think"—stepping in close behind me, Killian wrapped his arms around my waist, pulling my shirt free—"that we need to get you out of these wet clothes."

I met his eyes in the mirror as he rested his chin on my shoulder. "I think you may be right."

"Mmm. Good." Starting at the bottom of my shirt, he began to flick open the buttons, his gaze roving over my body as though he already had me good and naked. His skillful fingers made quick work of my shirt, and then he peeled it off my shoulders and down my arms slowly, teasing, drawing out the moment as he drank me in and pressed a kiss where my neck and shoulder met.

"You're unbelievably sexy, Levi Walker." Killian unbuttoned my pants and, as he drew the zipper down, said, "I hope you know I'm not going to let you go."

His words sent a shiver down my spine. Seconds later, he dipped his thumbs under my boxer briefs and then knelt behind me, pulling the rest of my clothes off me and discarding them by the door. When he didn't get up right away, I glanced over my shoulder to see him trailing his hands up the back of my calves, up the back of my thighs, and then my ass, where he paused and looked up at me.

Those blue eyes glittered with wicked desire, something that was now coursing through my body as well. Actually, I'd been ready to get Killian's hands back on me from the second I left his bed only a few short hours ago.

"So fucking sexy," Killian murmured against my skin, and then he rose to his feet and quickly stripped out of his shirt and jeans. Before I could turn around, he moved, pressing the front of his strong body against the back of mine, nestling his rock-hard cock against my ass.

I couldn't stop staring at the picture we made in the mirror. Killian was a beautiful force of nature, with dark hair long enough to grab on to, the long, built muscles from his time onstage, and those piercing blue eyes. What did he see when he looked at me?

As if he knew what I was thinking, a smirk crossed his lips. "Not so respectable without clothes, are you?" His arms circled my waist, and then he wrapped his hands around my cock, causing me to suck in a breath.

Slowly he began to stroke, keeping his eyes on mine in the mirror, watching the way I bit down on my lip from the feel of his hands on me.

I cursed under my breath as he drew out his movements, apparently keen to torture me tonight. "More," I said.

"More?" Killian stroked my dick a little faster as I pumped my hips to set the pace. "How much more do you want, Levi? Tell me."

"I want you to stop teasing me—" As soon as the words were out of my mouth, Killian dropped his hands and took a step back. I nearly fell over from the lack of him, and soon, my need turned to frustration as I whirled around to face him. "Dammit, Killian, I need—"

"What?" His expression darkened with hunger. "What is it you need?"

"Every bit of you I can get." Then I reached for him, holding both sides of his face between my hands as I stole a kiss. As ravenous as I was, his mouth opened to mine automatically, inviting me in. It wasn't slow, and it wasn't sweet. It was savage, both of us greedily taking what we wanted from each other. I was so lost in Killian's kiss that I didn't even notice when he backed me up against the sink.

Without breaking apart, he lifted me slightly, so I was sitting on the counter. The cold granite had me gasping against his mouth, making Killian chuckle as he sucked in my breath.

I wound my legs around him, and when I did, it brought his erection up against mine and, without thinking, I reached between us, taking our cocks in my hand and giving us a firm squeeze.

"Oh fuck," Killian said, planting his hands on the counter beside my thighs as his head fell back. "That. Keep doing that."

With his words a sexy as hell plea, I couldn't resist. Using our pre-cum as lube, I began to stroke, the friction of our cocks rubbing together so good my eyes rolled in the back of my head.

Killian let out a string of curses as he lifted his head, and then his mouth was on mine, matching the pace my hand set between us.

God, he felt good. So good. Too good. I'd known it could be like this if I ever allowed it to happen, and shit, maybe that was what scared me, because after Killian, who could possibly compare?

"*Mmm...*" The rumbling growl that escaped Killian had me moaning. "Lean back on the counter. Lemme look at you."

No longer able to deny him anything, let alone such a

provocative demand, I braced my palms on the cool surface behind me. Killian straightened to his full height, and his eyes cruised down my neck, my naked chest and abs, and then finally they landed on the cock standing at attention for him.

I widened my legs a fraction. Killian's gaze was so hot, so tangible, I was squirming on the counter, as I reached down and circled the base of my dick, angling it his way.

Killian's eyes climbed back up to mine. "Want something, Levi?"

"You know exactly what I want."

Killian's grin was arrogant, confident, and sexy, and I couldn't help but think how well suited we were. "Maybe. But I *really* want to hear you say it."

Never having been the shy, retiring type, I gave myself a couple of good, hard pulls, my body stretched out in a way that left little to nothing to the imagination, and then I gave him exactly what he'd asked for—the truth. "I want to fuck your mouth."

Killian reached down and fisted his length, and I added, "Then I want to come in it."

Something flashed in Killian's eyes then. Something hot and tumultuous, something sinful. It made goosebumps break out over my skin and fire lick through my veins, and when he moved back between my spread thighs and planted his hands on the counter by my hips, Killian leaned over me and said against my mouth, "Aren't you demanding tonight?"

I reached up and tangled my fingers through that gorgeous, thick hair of his, and tugged his head back so I could look him in the eye. "Complaining?"

"Not fucking ever."

"Good," I said, and then added some pressure to the back of his head, directing Killian exactly where I wanted him to go. "Then how about we give your mouth something else to do, so I don't make that mistake again?"

Killian chuckled, and his warm breath washed over the head of my cock, making me tremble.

"See? This is why you're my manager. Always coming up with the best way to keep me in line."

Somehow I had a feeling that would be the last thing I was going to come up with, because Killian was now tonguing the wet slit of my dick, and every other coherent thought in my brain had taken a lightning-fast detour south.

THIRTY-TWO

Killian

_____

SEEMED LIKE MY manager wanted to…*manage* me tonight, and hell if I had a problem with that. With the wanton way Levi was lounged back on the bathroom counter with his legs spread wide and his beautiful body on full display for me, I would willingly follow him to the end of the earth if that was where he wanted me to go.

Lucky for me, his wants were much less drastic than that—and much more pleasurable.

The fingers in my hair twisted, and the sharp sting of pain made my dick throb. Christ, from the second Levi had stepped inside my hotel suite, he'd been on a mission, and as I swirled my tongue around the swollen head of his dick, I felt confident that I was about to help him complete it.

A low groan escaped Levi, and he released his shaft to again brace himself on the counter. I curled my fingers around his engorged length and directed it my way, and as I lowered my mouth and sucked the tip of him between my lips, I aimed my eyes up to his.

The rampant lust swirling in Levi's eyes was a high like no

other, and when I increased the suction on his cock, he cursed and wound his leg around my back.

"Jesus, Killian… Stop fucking teasing me and suck it already."

The frustration in those words made my balls ache. I smoothed my hands along his thighs and raised my head, releasing him completely. Then I hooked my hand under the leg he had hiked up around me and brought it over my shoulder.

Levi gasped as he stumbled back a little further on the counter. But he quickly regained his balance where he now practically lay on the granite top. He was about as spread open and vulnerable as he could be, and as I kissed and licked my way up the inside of his thigh, the fingers in my hair tightened.

Fuck, he was as insatiable as I was.

Greedy, sexy, and demanding as hell. Levi was everything I'd ever wanted, and then I reached the V of his groin and nuzzled my nose in to take a long, deep inhale of his arousal.

"*Ahh…*" Levi panted when I dragged my tongue along the underside of his length, tracing the veins with the tip of my tongue. "Killian."

My name sounded like a prayer as it fell off his lips, and this time when I reached the head of his cock, I glanced up at him and said, "Give it to me."

Levi's nostrils flared, then he gripped my hair, dug his heel between my shoulder blades, and shoved up into my mouth with one solid thrust. He tunneled all the way inside until he nearly hit the back of my throat, and as Levi held me in place, my mouth completely full, I felt my climax threatening.

This wasn't going to last long at all.

"God*damn*," Levi said as his hips began to move. Then he was making quick, hard jabs in and out of my mouth with his cock, desperate for release.

I growled around the intrusion and ran my hands down to

his bare ass, and when he canted his hips up, and I grabbed a handful of each curve, Levi got the message.

The exact same one he'd relayed to me earlier: *More. Give me more.*

So he did.

With one hand directing my head, and my hands helping him to move in and out, Levi's legs anchored him, in what was the hottest, most intense face fuck of my life. And I loved every damn minute of it.

"Fuck. Oh fuck, Killian. That's…"

Exactly. There were no words for how damn good this was, and as Levi leaned back against the mirror so he could bring both hands to my hair, I knew he was getting close.

He was done watching, done giving demands—now it was all about closing his eyes and feeling the rush, the high, the sublime ecstasy of being with the one who matched you in all the right ways.

My jaw ached from the pounding it was getting, but I didn't give a fuck as Levi bottomed out and tensed under my hands, and when his ass cheeks clenched and his body began to tremble, I glanced up just in time to see him shout my name as he came hot and hard on my tongue.

He was the most spectacular sight I'd seen in my life, and as he began to still and I drew my lips off him, Levi's eyes slowly opened and I knew I was done for.

He was it for me, one hundred percent it, and it took everything I had not to say it when my emotions were dying to spill out of me. But I would wait; I would let him get used to the idea of us the way I had. The last thing I wanted was to freak him out by pushing him too fast.

I straightened up and Levi unwound himself. I grabbed his hand and hauled him up until he was again seated on the edge of the counter. Gripping his chin in my hand, I pressed my lips to his, and when he shoved his tongue into my mouth, the knowledge he was tasting himself on my tongue was almost more than my still-very-*aroused* cock could handle.

"So," Levi said, his chest heaving a little as his breathing came back to normal. "How was your...cake?"

I tugged him off the counter until he was standing and pulled him toward the shower. "Best fuckin' chocolate cake I've ever eaten. I can't wait to have more."

"Greedy."

I turned on the shower, and as the water heated, I brushed a kiss over his lips and said, "With you, I'm downright insatiable."

Levi grinned and reached for my cock. "Charmer."

I flashed him my most *charming* smile, and Levi chuckled as he gave me a firm stroke.

"But it won't work with me. It's my turn." With a smirk on his full lips, Levi released me, and I whimpered. "Get in the shower, Killian. You're not the only one who believes in having his cake and eating it too."

THIRTY-THREE

Killian

"YO, ASSHOLE! OVER here!"

As I stepped out onto the terrace of the cafe Viper had told me to meet him at, I drank in the sight of the new city that greeted us—Brisbane. This was the final leg of the world tour, and tonight was our final show.

To say I was feeling good would be the understatement of the century. With Levi in my bed each night, his eyes on me whenever I hit the stage, the world I'd seen several times over had taken on a whole new dynamic this time around—one I knew I'd remember for years to come.

Tugging my baseball cap low across my forehead, I wove my way through the bustling tables and headed to where Viper was seated. Clearly not in a hurry to attract attention either, Viper had dressed much like myself—jeans, t-shirt, sunglasses, and a baseball cap.

"'Bout time you showed up," Viper said, as he leaned back in his seat and kicked his long legs out in front of himself. "Thought I might have to send out a search party."

"I'm not that fucking late."

Viper looked at me over the top of his glasses. "Five minutes late is like an hour for you. Not that you'd be that difficult to find. These days you're either in Levi's suite or *in* Levi himself. Find him, find you. Really, you two need to step up your stealth game."

I snorted and shot him the finger. "Like you did when it came to Halo? Sure. Like we didn't all know you were...*into* him before you told us."

Viper's lips quirked at the sides. "Yeah, well, I wasn't exactly trying to keep it a secret. The first song I wrote for him to sing was called 'Hard.' If you morons hadn't worked it out from that, I'd have needed to go and invest in some Viagra for the lot of you."

"Well, let me be the first to inform you that I am in no need of *that*."

"Not now, you're not. But for a while there I was starting to worry." Viper picked up the menu and flicked it open. "You weren't bringing anyone round, you were grumpier than a bear with a thorn in its paw, and honestly, the moon-eyed way you look at Levi makes even *my* 'in love' self want to gag."

I knew Viper was probably right when it came to the way I looked at Levi. Hell, it was difficult to hide your feelings when what was causing them was always so close by. But if Levi caught wind that others around us could see just how hard I had fallen for him, he would more than likely pull back.

Sure, he'd told me he was okay with the rest of the guys knowing that we were together. But it wasn't lost on me that neither of us had made the move to fill them in, and Viper hadn't either. Instead, whenever the other band members were nearby, Levi made sure to keep his hands to himself, and an appropriate distance between the two of us.

He chalked that up to us being able to have a relationship and still be professional, but I knew there was much more to it than that. I had to tread carefully if I wanted this to go all the way, and with the horror story of Jonny never far from my mind, I knew I needed to change topics with Viper now before he had me saying shit I shouldn't. Like just how badly I wanted the world to know that Levi was mine.

"So, new music. Let's talk," I said, after the two of us placed our orders. "That one you were working on, it still flowing for you?"

Viper refilled his coffee mug and nodded. "Yeah, it is. I gotta say"—he took a sip of the hot brew and flashed a crooked grin—"feels good to be hearing things again."

I chuckled. "When you talk like that, you sound like you need to be committed. Or, at the very least, medicated."

"Hey, meds might help, you don't know."

"Like we need you any fucking crazier than you already are. Knowing our luck, you'd start hallucinating and wind up in the papers running naked down a street or some shit."

"Nah," Viper said, as he looked out at the city skyline. "There's no way in hell Halo will let anyone but him see me naked ever again. He'd chain me to the bed first."

"An image I really could've done without," I told him, then took a sip of the orange juice sitting in front of me. "So about this song of yours."

"Yeah, right. I've got most of the chorus, I'm just looking for some lead-in lyrics and the hook. Thought you might wanna work on it with me. You know, like the old days."

"The old days?" I laughed. "Are we even old enough to *have* old days."

"Okay, how about the TBD days?"

"Better," I said as the waiter arrived with my poached eggs on toast and Viper's Aussie scramble. After we thanked him and he headed off, I picked up my knife and fork. "You don't want to finish this one with Halo?"

Viper reached for the hot sauce and shook it. "We've been working on a couple already, but we were both just saying how it would be great to have your influence on this next album.

You have such a distinctive voice, man. Our fans would go crazy for a few new Killian songs to scream at the top of their fuckin' lungs. Hell, so would I."

It was funny. I knew Viper was thinking of our harder-hitting powerhouse songs that used to rattle stadium seats. But the song I wanted to show him today was nothing like that. It was more a power *ballad*. One I could imagine Halo crooning to a packed stadium of fans waving their hands in the air as they sang along and made out with the person beside them.

"I can definitely get on board with that. But the one I want to show you today, it's more mellow than you're probably thinking of."

"I'm down for mellow, as long as it's not some whiny, depressive shit you wrote while pining after our manager."

"Bite me."

"Eh, I don't know," Viper said, and then waggled his eyebrows. "Levi might get pissed if he sees me nibbling on you. Not to mention Halo…"

Fucking gross. While ninety-nine percent of the human population would sell their soul to have Viper's mouth on them, I'd known the bastard way too long and been through way too much to think of him in any other way than…brotherly.

"Excuse me while I go and bleach my brain to get rid of *that* particular image." Viper flashed a toothy grin, making me grimace. "Seriously, stop with the teeth shit. You're gonna give me nightmares."

Viper started laughing hard, and then shoveled a forkful of food in his mouth. The two of us then cleaned off half our plates before talking again.

"So, okay," Viper said. "This song you been working on. You bring it with you?"

I dug my hand into my pocket and pulled out the folded piece of paper with the lyrics I'd thought of back in Sydney. After tossing it on the table between us, I reached for my discarded knife, and when I noticed my hand shaking, I frowned.

What the hell was the matter with me? I was never nervous when it came to shit like this. I'd known Viper my entire life, been working on music with him for most of it, and never had my stomach twisted around on itself when I gave him something to read. My general feelings in the past were always: if he didn't like something, fuck him. He wasn't the authority. But for some reason, I really wanted him to like this piece.

A couple minutes passed, but it might as well have been an hour with how quiet Viper was being, then he raised his eyes to mine and let out a low whistle.

"Damn, Kill."

Oh shit, he hated it.

"This is…" As Viper's words trailed off, I held my breath. "This is some fuckin' love song right here, man. Has Levi seen this yet? Have you played it for him?"

Wait…what? No.

Viper had it all wrong. It wasn't a *love* song, per se. It was more about lust, and giving in to emotions that had been building over time. It was about finally allowing yourself to see, and fall into the arms of the one who had been right in front of you all along. As in fall into *bed*. Not love.

"It's not a love song, and no, I haven't shown him. Why would I?" I said, taking on a defensive tone that I couldn't quite control. "This isn't about us. It's more…general than that. You know, for anyone who's ever had feelings for someone but couldn't act on them."

"Like you and Levi."

"Like you and fucking Halo," I countered.

"Mhmm." Viper sat back in his chair and reached for his sunglasses, slowly drawing them off. "I'm not judging you. I told you it was something else. It's really fuckin' beautiful, actually. But it's pretty obvious who it's about."

I rolled my eyes and snatched the paper back, reading over the lyrics. "No," I said, shaking my head. "I generalized. If you're picking up on anything it's because you know me, that's all."

"So it *is* about Levi."

"Drop it, Viper."

"I'm just saying, if I picked up on it…"

Letting out a sigh, I pinched the bridge of my nose. "It's not like that with us, okay?" Lie. That was such a fucking lie.

"Okaaay. But Kill?"

"What?"

"It's totally like that." As I glared across the table at Viper, he said, "How long have we known each other?"

"Too fucking long, I'm starting to realize as I sit here."

"Whatever," Viper said. "Who was the first person to tell me to pull my head out of my ass when it came to Halo?"

Yeah, okay, that'd been me.

"And who was the first person to point out that I never acted the way I was—all in love and shit—*until* Halo?"

Yeah…that'd also been me.

"We've known each other too long and too well not to see the signs, man. And all I'm saying is, you better show Levi that song before he hears Halo sing it to the rest of the world. He's smart, Killian. He's going to know you wrote it about him. Trust me."

Shit, was it really that obvious? I thought I'd been subtle. I thought I'd made it general enough that it could be about anyone. There was no way Levi was going to let a song that blatantly told the world how I felt about him be blasted out to millions of people. *Fuck.*

"You're wrong," I said, refolding the paper and shoving it back in my pocket.

Viper scoffed. "No, I'm not."

"Yes, you fucking are," I said, suddenly annoyed and not

having a clue why. "Unlike you and the angel, not everyone who sleeps together is madly in love. In fact, some of us are just doing it because it feels really good, and it's easier than having to go out and find someone different whenever we hit a new city. So get off my ass, okay? Levi knows exactly what's going on between us, and I can tell you right now, it's not some great love affair."

Even as the words left my mouth, I knew them to be the lie they were. I didn't want a great love affair with Levi; I wanted a forever love affair with him. But when Viper said nothing, and his eyes rose up over my shoulder and widened, the hair on the back of my neck rose.

No. No, no, please, God, no. Don't let who I think is standing behind me—

"Levi," Viper said.

—be standing behind me.

I let out a silent curse and squeezed my eyes shut. *This* could not be happening.

"Um, would you like to join us?" Viper said, but the awkward delivery made it clear that whatever he was reading on Levi's face said the last thing he wanted was to be anywhere near us—me in particular, I was guessing.

When all that met Viper was stony silence, I turned in my chair, holding on to some kind of misguided hope that I hadn't just fucked up the best thing that had ever happened to me by trying to throw Viper's gossipy ass off the scent. But as soon as I caught sight of Levi's expression, I knew I was out of luck.

I thought I'd seen Levi's every emotion. Anger, happiness, arousal, and annoyance. But as I zeroed in on his stunning face now, I realized there was one emotion I hadn't seen on him before—betrayal—and the devastation swirling in those beautiful dark eyes of his were like someone plunging a knife right through my heart.

Jesus, this could not be fucking happening to me.

As I shoved my chair back and got to my feet, Levi spun on his heel, clearly about to make a beeline out of there without saying a word. I could feel the eyes of the other diners on us now, but I didn't give a shit. And as he took a step forward, I reached out and grabbed hold of his arm, halting him.

Levi glanced down at my hand and said, "Let me go."

"Levi—"

"I said, let. Me. Go."

He was practically vibrating with emotions—none of which were good, I was sure—and as I slowly removed my hand, I heard him say, "Stay away from me."

Before I could tell him that this was all a colossal misunderstanding, that I hadn't meant what I'd said and had just been blowing Viper off, Levi stormed out of the café, leaving me standing there surrounded by strangers—and suddenly, that felt like the loneliest place in the entire world.

THIRTY-FOUR

Killian

LEVI HADN'T SAID a word to me in almost twenty-four hours. After overhearing the conversation with Viper, he'd simply vanished, refusing to answer his phone or come to the door. I didn't know if he was even at the hotel, and Liam wasn't around either.

I'd fucked up. Obviously I hadn't wanted to tell Viper how deep I was falling, not when I hadn't even told Levi. And there was no telling Levi only to scare him off. So I'd lied through my teeth, brushing off Viper's questions with a nonchalance I didn't feel. I hadn't expected Levi to hear what I said, but now he had and now he thought he was a casual fuck, which was the furthest thing from my mind.

He had to know better, though. Right?

As I loaded my bags into the trunk of the van picking us up for our flight home, a hand clapped down on my shoulder. Viper.

"Anything?" he asked, and I shook my head. "I haven't seen him either."

I sighed, shoving my carry-on into a tight space bookended

by two massive Louis Vuitton suitcases, which could only be Jagger's. "It's fine. I'll fix it."

"Gonna be an awkward flight home if you don't."

"Yeah, no shit."

I glanced around, looking for Levi, but he hadn't come down with us, which was odd for him, considering he always wanted to make sure everyone got to our destinations in one piece.

Taking a seat in the front row of the van, I kept the space beside me open as the rest of the guys and Imogen filed in and took up the remaining rows. I tapped my fingers along the armrest as I watched the front of the hotel for Levi's familiar shock of blond hair.

Surely he was coming, right? He always flew with us, and it'd be crazy to buy a seat on a different jet.

Before I could stress over that too much, Levi walked out of the hotel with his bag and Liam beside him. The first thing I noticed were the blue and yellow checkered pants, because how the hell he pulled off such loud outfits and still looked so fucking gorgeous was beyond me, but it worked for him. *More than works for him*, I thought, biting down on my lip as I watched him approach, pants riding low on his hips.

The second thing I noticed was the lack of a pissed-off expression on his face, thank fuck, which made a flicker of hope light up inside me. Maybe things weren't as off track as I feared.

The door to the van was yanked open suddenly, and there he was. Levi leaned inside, scanning his eyes over us as if making sure everyone was accounted for, but it didn't escape my notice that when he got to me, he looked over my head, avoiding my gaze completely.

"Liam," Levi called out, nodding for him to get in the van. Liam took the spot I'd saved for Levi. Levi slammed the door shut and then hopped in the front passenger seat.

Guess the whole "no pissed-off expression" was more of a sign of professionalism and less what he was feeling on the inside.

Yep. I was fucked.

The radio blasted the whole way to the airport, and then Levi was the first one out of the van, practically sprinting through security to stay away from me. He didn't turn around when I called his name, and he wasn't in the lounge with the rest of us waiting to board.

Fucking great. Viper had been dead-on when he said the plane ride home would be awkward. I couldn't exactly have the talk I wanted to with a bunch of eavesdropping assholes around, could I?

Beside me, Halo sat on the edge of Viper's armchair, reading over the lyrics we'd worked on yesterday and making notes in pencil in the margins. Every so often, he'd look up at where Imogen stood with Slade and Jagger, the three of them off in their own little world, and I wondered if he'd clued in yet to what was obviously happening there. I sure as hell wasn't looking forward to the day when he figured out his innocent little sister wasn't so innocent at all—at least not with those guys—and though I didn't know specifics, their body language said more than I cared to know. Hell, Jagger wasn't even being subtle, not with the way he fingered her necklace that definitely hadn't been there when she arrived in Australia.

Thank God Halo—and Viper, apparently—were oblivious, because—

"What the *fuck*?" Halo slapped the papers in his hand onto Viper's lap, his focus never leaving the threesome as he marched across the room, his fists curling at his sides.

Oh shit.

Before he could say a word, Viper and I were on our feet.

"What the hell is goin' on here?" Halo spat, but as Imogen started to answer, he held up his hand. "And don't tell me nothing, because I'm not fucking blind. Don't think I haven't noticed how much time you've been spending with these two, Im."

"Who am I supposed to spend time with, then? You? I couldn't pull you away from Viper for a day if I tried."

Halo reared back like he'd been slapped. "That's not true. I always have time for you."

Imogen shrugged, her long red hair falling over her shoulder. "Maybe, maybe not. But don't get pissed at Slade and Jagger. They haven't done anything wrong."

"Bullshit," Viper said under his breath, low enough that only I could hear.

He was right: Slade was looking guilty as shit standing there, rubbing the back of his neck as he looked at Jagger as if asking what the fuck they should do. He might look like an intimidating fucker, but if anyone else in this band was a lover, not a fighter besides me, it was Slade. Before five seconds ago I would've said Halo, but he looked out to kill, so...

Run, if you're smart, I thought, as Halo turned to Slade and crossed his arms. "That true, Slade? You and Im just friends? Nothing you need to confess?"

Slade swallowed hard, his eyes nervously darting between Imogen and Jagger, who both looked cool as cucumbers, even if the sweat on their brows was starting to give them away.

"We're friends," Slade finally said.

"*Special* friends?" Viper asked.

"Get outta here with that shit," Jagger said, pushing Viper's chest so he was forced to take a step back.

"Don't fucking touch me. Unless you wanna be facedown on the ground in about two seconds."

"Threats now, V? You wanna defend your boy's honor?" Jagger snorted and then lifted his chin toward Halo. "I don't think he needs your guard dog services, so you can back off."

Viper took a menacing step forward, but Halo shot his arm out, holding Viper back, but just barely.

"How about you three answer the question," Halo said, patience running low.

Imogen rolled her eyes. "This is ridiculous. You're overreacting over nothing."

"I don't think it's nothing."

"Halo—"

"Tell me what the fuck is going on," Halo roared, the unexpected booming sound of his voice echoing off the walls. I'd never seen the angel so worked up; his skin was turning a deep red, and there was a vicious snarl on his face.

It was a long moment before Jagger held his hands up and sighed. "Fine. You wanna know what's goin' on? The same thing that's been goin' on since Paris."

Panic crossed Imogen's face. "Jagger, no—"

"I care about your sister." Jagger placed an arm around her waist and drew her into his side, and not a second later, Slade did the same on her other side. "We're together. All of us."

Halo's eyes darted between the three of them, and then he stumbled back. "What…what did you just say?"

Imogen's head fell into her hands. "Oh God."

"You heard me," Jagger said, a clear challenge in those dark eyes. "You may not like it, but I'm tired of having to hide shit from you."

"Yeah," Slade said, squaring his shoulders. "This is how it is. We love her."

A gasp left Imogen, and then she looked up at Slade. "What? You do?"

A smile slowly stretched across Slade's face as he nodded, and then on her other side, Jagger said, "I do too."

"Oh my God." Imogen's voice cracked as she looked between her lovers with tears in her eyes.

It would've been an incredibly romantic moment if they'd

kept that shit hidden, locked away in a hotel room, but they couldn't make things easy, could they?

They were so lost in each other, no one in their threesome noticed the way smoke practically poured out of Halo's ears.

I knew what was coming, but I wasn't close enough to stop it, and it all happened so fast that there was no time for a warning.

With a growl that ripped out of his chest and echoed off the walls, beast Halo fucking *attacked*.

THIRTY-FIVE

Levi

___

I WAS GONE for twenty minutes to grab some food with Liam, but that was all it took for World War III to break out.

When I walked into the private lounge, the view that greeted me was one I'd seen before, but always with other bands, never with Fallen Angel.

Halo had a fistful of Jagger's shirt, his arm cocked back as both Imogen and Slade tried to stop him, but he threw the punch fast, the knock against Jagger's jaw one I heard across the room.

"Shit," I said, tossing my food onto a nearby table and rushing toward the madness.

Chaos broke out. Jagger went to retaliate against Halo, but Viper shoved him away. Slade grabbed Imogen and quickly moved her out of the way before diving in, heading straight for Viper and putting him in a headlock. Killian moved fast, working to separate Viper and Slade, while Imogen shouted for everyone to chill their tits.

Jesus, where to even start.

"Why would you mess with my sister, you asshole?" Halo had his arms around Jagger's waist, trying to get him on the ground, but it wasn't until Jagger knocked into the others, losing his balance, that Halo succeeded.

Halo straddled Jagger's waist, throwing blows that Jagger struggled to fend off.

"Yo, this may be the way you like it, but this position doesn't work for me," Jagger yelled, arching up to try to throw Halo off. Then, because he was an idiot who wanted to fan the flames, he added, "It only works with your sister."

Aaand that's where to start.

"You fucking bastard—" Halo went to pound Jagger's face, but I reached them just in time, grabbing Halo's arms and lifting him just enough that Jagger was able to wriggle out from beneath him. Imogen was there in a flash, checking Jagger's face as he assured her he was fine.

With Halo's arms pinned behind his back, he was at an awkward angle, but the guy was hyped on adrenaline and stronger than I expected.

He broke free again, heading straight for Jagger. Imogen put her hands up, trying to get him to stop, but Jagger was ready, and the two of them went tumbling around on the floor.

"Halo, stop, I'm not a kid—" Imogen's voice got lost in the pandemonium, and to my right, Killian had lost his hold on Viper and Slade after one of them accidentally knocked him in the jaw with their elbow. Rattled, Killian stepped back for a second, rubbing his jaw.

I'd rather have been the one knocking him senseless. I still couldn't believe what he'd said to Viper, how he'd blown me off so casually, as if I didn't matter. It had hurt. It had hurt like hell, and it still did. But I didn't have time to think about that now.

Killian looked up at me, and it was impossible to miss the apology in his eyes, but I didn't want to hear how sorry he was for getting caught.

When Viper plowed Slade into the wall with a loud *boom*

and Slade landed an uppercut on Viper, everything between Killian and me was put on the backburner. We had to get this situation under control, or there was no way we'd be heading back to the States today…at least not with anyone alive.

"Should I call for help?" Liam asked from behind me.

"No," Killian answered. "You two deal with Halo and Viper, and I'll get the others the hell out of here."

I gave him a curt nod and turned to Liam. "Get rough if you need to." My brother was no slouch in the ass-kicking department, but I knew he wouldn't want to hurt a member of one of his favorite bands.

Too bad, I thought, letting him deal with beast Halo this time as I snuck up behind Viper, who still had Slade up against the wall, and wrapped my arms around him. I jerked us back hard, hard enough that we half fell onto one of the couches.

Viper let out a howl of frustration, but I held tight to him.

Liam had somehow grabbed hold of Halo and was pinning him to the ground as Killian freed Jagger.

"Fuck your face," Halo shouted as Jagger got to his feet. Even struggling beneath my brother, he was spouting off insults. Then Halo's eyes narrowed on Slade. "And fuck you too, man. You mother*fuckers*. That's my baby sister you're messing with—"

"That's enough." Liam pressed his knee higher up on Halo's spine, cutting off his words. The expression on my brother's face told me he was worried about incurring the Fallen Angel singer's wrath for what he was doing, but it was that or watch these guys fight to the death over something they could talk out eventually.

I hoped, anyway.

"You three," Killian said, pointing to Slade, Jagger, and Imogen. "Out."

"Going." Imogen grabbed both the guys' hands, pulling

them toward the door, but they dragged their feet until Killian brought up the rear, forcing them out.

When the door slammed shut, I dropped my hold on Viper, but Liam kept Halo on the ground.

"You sure it's safe?" Liam asked. When I shrugged—because honestly, who knew at this point—Liam cautiously stood up.

Viper practically rolled off the couch, his joints cracking in protest the same way all of ours were, and made his way over to Halo, who was still lying on the floor, his head in his hands.

"Angel," Viper said quietly, running his fingers through Halo's blond curls. "You okay?"

Halo shook his head, not saying a word. I took the silence as an opportunity to sit up and survey the damage.

Nothing broken in the room, at least, and hopefully no broken bones on any of the guys.

Liam stopped in front of me and grinned. "Don't think I've ever seen you such a mess, bro."

I looked down at where half my shirt was untucked and I seemed to be missing a button or two. "First time for everything. Thanks for helping."

"I'm gonna be banned from their shows now, huh?"

"Nah, they'll get over it."

I looked over to where Viper had Halo in his arms. It seemed like the anger was still there, but neither of them were making a move to go after the others, so that was a win in my book.

Relationships. That was what caused ninety-five percent of issues within every damn band on the planet. Who was fucking who, who wasn't, who was with who, who was left out…it was exhausting. It was yet another reason I'd shied away from ever getting involved with anyone after Jonny.

But no, I'd thrown every logical thought out the window

with Killian's sweet talk and with what I'd thought was genuine interest, backed up by genuine actions.

I'd been a fool. Slade and Jagger were fools too. They *knew* Halo's sister was off-limits, but of course a challenge was exactly what guys like them wanted.

"This," I said, standing up so I could glare at Halo and Viper. When they looked up, I shook my head and started to pace. "This is why inter-band relationships don't work. It's messy as hell. Nothing lasts forever, so when it all comes crashing down, guess what happens? It all goes to shit. Everything you've worked so hard for destroyed because no one can keep it in their goddamn pants."

Halo blinked at me. Viper raised his brow.

"You think you can make it work now, but when are you all going to understand it never works. Huh?" When no one answered—not that I expected them to—I went on. "You're on borrowed time. This? It never lasts. It can't. Temptation is fucking everywhere, there's always some new shiny toy to play with, and then the next thing you know, you're tossed aside. Forgotten." I stopped, the realization I'd gone too far crossing my mind. I'd veered into personal territory, put my fears on the one couple that probably *would* make it if anyone could.

I let out a deep sigh, one that spoke of how damn mentally exhausted I was.

"Nice speech," Viper said. "Is that why you're running?"

"What?" I reared back, Viper's words slapping me in the face. "I'm not running."

How could I run from something Killian didn't even want? It made no sense.

Viper shrugged, but his eyes were all too knowing. "Sure, Levi. You keep telling yourself that."

THIRTY-SIX

Killian

WE'D BEEN BACK in New York for two days when I decided forty-eight hours was enough time for Levi to get over the jet lag and, hopefully, be open enough to give me a chance to explain.

I was still recovering from the plane ride from hell, the extremely tense trip from Brisbane to L.A. to New York. No one had said a word to each other the entire time, but if looks could kill, we would all be dead. I, for one, was just grateful we'd made it back to the States in one piece. Everyone needed a few days to cool off, but I felt confident that when the fires burned out, we'd all be able to come together and laugh it off.

Well, I felt *reasonably* confident about that.

With my hands in my pockets, I strolled down Wooster Street, toward Levi's place in Soho. I'd never actually been there before; we'd always had meetings at my place, which seemed to be the general gathering spot for the band. But Levi had mentioned enough about the area he lived in that it didn't take a genius to do some snooping and find out his exact address.

I came to a stop in front of the long, cream-colored doors. I wasn't sure if I'd even walk inside past them, because there was a huge chance Levi wouldn't ask me up when I hit the buzzer for his apartment. But seeing as he still wouldn't answer or return my calls, I had to give it a shot.

Blowing out a breath, I walked over to the intercom and glanced at the short list of names. There he was: L. Walker, Apt. 3B

Here goes nothin'.

The front door of the building burst open beside me as someone walked out, and I didn't hesitate. I darted inside before it closed and headed up the three flights of stairs.

Good. I was already inside, so at least I wouldn't be standing on the street if Levi decided not to hear me out.

As I reached the third floor, I stopped, catching my breath. Not from exertion, but from the nerves suddenly flooding my system. *If any of the guys could see me now,* I thought, almost laughing to myself. *Not such a badass, am I?*

I cracked my neck from side to side and steeled myself as I headed toward 3B. *He'll understand. He'll listen, it'll all work out, and then we can laugh this off too.*

Before I could talk myself out of it, I rapped on Levi's door and stepped back to wait.

And wait.

And wait.

Shit, what if he wasn't even home? I hadn't counted on that. It would just be my luck if—

The door cracked open an inch, the chain still on so that only a sliver of Levi was showing. If he was surprised to see me there, his expression gave nothing away. Instead, he looked indifferent. "What do you want, Killian?"

I'd expected pissed off. What greeted me now was much worse.

Yeah, this wouldn't be easy.

I shoved my hands in my pockets. "Can we talk?"

"I think you've said enough."

"Not to you. Not to your face."

"Seriously? You came here just to tell me how inconsequential we were? There's no need to bother; I got the message loud and clear."

"No, you heard what I told Viper. You didn't hear the truth."

"The truth." Levi laughed derisively. "Or what you want me to hear?"

Footsteps pounded up the stairs, and as I looked over my shoulder, I sighed. "Can I come in? Please? I'd rather not have all of New York listening in on a private conversation."

Levi stared at me for a long moment and then shut the door in my face. A few seconds later, he'd unlatched the chain and opened the door, sweeping his hand inside for me to enter like it was the last thing he wanted.

I thought nothing could surprise me when it came to Levi, but I hadn't expected him to live in an artist's loft. The living area had stringed lights that hung across the exposed wooden beams, and the furniture was tasteful yet as bold as the man himself. There were splashes of bright colors everywhere—the deep red velvet couches, the abstract artwork on the walls. It was a hundred percent Levi, and when I turned around to face him, I told him as much.

He nodded and then crossed his arms over his chest, not offering for me to sit down or asking if I wanted a drink, something I had no doubt his hospitable self would've done in a heartbeat if he'd intended me to stay. He wanted me to say my piece and get the hell out.

Uphill battle it is.

I decided to start things out by admitting the first truth. "I fucked up."

Levi raised an eyebrow but stayed silent.

"And before you assume, I'll tell you all the ways I fucked up."

That got his attention. "There's more than just the one?"

"I shouldn't have talked to Viper about us. Period. What happens between us should stay there, and for that, I apologize."

"I don't care that you talked to Viper. Tell him whatever you want."

"That's just it. I couldn't do that. I couldn't tell Viper how I feel about you when I haven't even told you." When Levi didn't react, I went on. "You told me about your past, about Jonny. The last thing I wanted was for you to think I don't care about you—"

"Really? And that's how you show it? By telling Viper you're with me because it's easier than finding some stranger to get laid instead?"

"What was the alternative? To admit how much I was falling for you? It's none of Viper's business, so yeah, I lied. I lied to get him the fuck off my back, and that's what you happened to hear instead of the truth. And for that, I'm sorry, Levi. I'm so very sorry."

The silence that fell between us was one I couldn't read. Levi's expression betrayed nothing, and he sure as hell wasn't accepting my apology. He simply stared at me, like he was trying to see inside my head to find out if what I was saying was real, and the fact that he even had to wonder stung more than I would've believed possible.

THIRTY-SEVEN

Levi

_____

"HOW DO YOU think it felt," I said slowly, measuring my words, "to hear you say one thing to me and tell your best friend something completely different? Why would I believe you? You've known Viper for, what, over thirty years? You think I don't know you tell each other everything?"

"Almost everything," Killian said, but I waved him off.

"Don't bother."

"Don't— What do you mean don't bother?" Killian's brow furrowed. "I'm trying to explain here—"

"And I don't want to hear it. In fact, I think you might've actually done me a favor." Up until this point I'd managed to keep my distance from Killian, something I'd known was crucial for my sanity and heart. But as I stood there with the perfect opportunity to tell him that getting involved with him had been the biggest mistake of my life, I couldn't seem to get the lie I'd rehearsed over and over again to roll off my tongue.

"A favor?" Killian said, as an emotion I refused to acknowledge—something akin to hurt—flashed in his eyes.

"Right. I always knew getting involved with a client would be a mistake—"

"I'm not just some fucking client, Levi."

"Aren't you?" I schooled my features, as Killian took a step forward.

"No, I'm not, and you know it."

"I don't know anything of the sort. The last thing I heard was that I was nothing more than a casual *fuck*. So if that's the case, I guess that makes you nothing more than my client."

Killian's hand whipped out so fast that I didn't even see it coming, and before I knew it, he had my chin between his fingers and his mouth was hovering over the top of mine. A shiver raced up my spine from being so close to him again, and as I met his stare head-on, the hurt from seconds ago vanished, and in its place was something I couldn't quite decipher, something fiery.

"Tell me, Levi. Do all of your clients make you tremble like this?"

I swallowed around the lump that had formed in the back of my throat and reached up to take hold of Killian's arm. My intention was to shove his hand away, but the second my fingers touched his warm skin, they tightened around his wrist, where I could feel his pulse racing.

"Do they make your heart pound and your knees want to give way?"

No, they didn't, and as Killian's lips ghosted along my jaw to my ear, I held on a little tighter.

"Because that's what you do to me. Every time I see you, think about you, hell, every time I close my eyes and fucking dream about you. You make my heart pound and my knees go weak."

My eyes fluttered shut under the spell Killian was weaving, and when he lowered his forehead to mine and said, "I'm sorry," I felt myself beginning to cave. I could feel his warm breath on my lips, as he cradled my cheek, and when he guided my mouth up to meet his, I blindly followed.

The first touch was gentle, a test to see what I would allow, and being the fool that I was, I parted my lips and let him inside. Just one more taste, I told myself, just one more touch. But the second Killian's tongue found mine, I realized my mistake.

I'd had days to free myself from Killian Michaels, and within five minutes of being in his company, I'd given in to him again like the addict I was.

As he slid his fingers into my hair to angle my head for a deeper connection, I moaned into Killian's delicious mouth and melted into his touch. Every move he made was designed to tear apart my resolve to steer clear of this man. But when he moved his arm to wrap it around my waist, I placed my palms on his chest and none too gently pushed him away.

"Stop," I said, my breathing coming a little faster now as I took a step back, hoping the distance would also bring a little clarity.

As Killian's eyes found mine, I saw the lust and desire swirling in them. But lust wasn't enough, and I wasn't about to put myself back in a position where I would ultimately end up hurt.

"Why? It's pretty obvious you want me as much as I want you. Why are you being so stubborn about this?"

He wasn't wrong, which was infuriating, but instead of responding, I crossed my arms and gritted my teeth, "if you haven't got something nice to say" running through my head.

"I said I was sorry," Killian said, and rubbed his face. "What more can I do?"

I touched my fingers to my lips where Killian had just kissed me, and thought it was a shame that that would be the last time I'd ever taste him. But this was the way it had to be. It was the best for both of us. I'd known that from the beginning, but Killian had just been too damn tempting to resist.

"Nothing," I finally said. "There's nothing you can do or

say, Killian. It's better this way. Better that it ended now instead of months down the track, when I was picking out china patterns for us and you were busy looking for a way out."

"Wow." All color drained from Killian's face as he stared at me, the hurt re-entering his eyes. "You really do think I'm a piece of shit, don't you?"

"Killian I—"

"No," he said, and held a hand up. "I'm finally starting to get it." Shaking his head, Killian reached into his pocket and pulled out a folded piece of paper. "You know, I've done a lot of things in my life that I regret. Stupid shit, you know? But I never thought you'd end up being one of them."

As Killian tossed the paper down on my coffee table, he added, "This is what Viper and I were talking about that day in the cafe. It's a song I wrote after the first night I spent with you in Sydney."

Killian turned on his heel and walked to my front door. He pulled it open, stopped in the doorway, looked back over his shoulder, and said, "He told me it was a love song. Stupid, huh?"

Then, without another word, he walked out the door.

THIRTY-EIGHT

Killian

THERE WAS NO way in hell I was going home after leaving Levi's place. I figured if I had to be miserable anywhere, I might as well drown my sorrows in the bottom of a bottle at a dive bar I frequented with the guys.

Only tonight I sat at the bar alone, wishing like hell I could have a redo on today. But maybe that wouldn't have made a difference, since Levi seemed pretty set on his decision to leave *us* completely in the past.

Such a stubborn fucker, I thought, swirling the contents of my fourth bourbon as I sat having a pity party for one. I'd tried to make it a pity party for two, but there wasn't one person in the bar my dick had sat up and paid any attention to. Just my luck.

I swallowed down the rest of my drink and raised the glass for another. *Just keep 'em comin',* I'd told the bartender when I sat down, and I had a feeling no matter how drunk I got, he wouldn't cut me off. After all, I was Killian Michaels, and who would say no to me?

Fuckin' Levi Walker, that was who.

Deciding I'd had enough of my own damn company, I fished my cell out of my pocket and called someone I knew would be able to commiserate with my shit luck. Or at least someone who'd get drunk with me and then probably tell me to shove my problems back up my ass.

Twenty minutes later, Viper planted his ass on the barstool beside me, where I already had a glass of whiskey waiting for him. He didn't say anything as he drank, his eyes glued to the TV over the bar, where a rerun of *Seinfeld* played. Once he'd finished off round one and gotten a refill, he finally acknowledged my presence.

"Smacked the fuck down again. How's it feel?"

"Fuck you," I replied.

"Eh, if it's all the same to you, I think I'm gonna pass. If Levi kicked you to the curb, you've obviously lost your touch."

"I haven't lost my touch." I stared down into the amber liquor and gave it another swirl. "Shit, maybe I have."

"You're not surrounded by any enticing alternatives, so, yeah, you're fucked."

I shot Viper a glare. "Thanks."

"Just tellin' it like it is. Assuming that's why you called me and not Slade."

Ignoring that, I took a drink and then swiveled on the barstool so I could check out the new arrivals. Following my lead, Viper did the same.

As I scanned the room, I could feel the mounting disappointment—not one person in the entire bar did anything for me, and what that meant was nothing good.

"What about the ginger at two o'clock?" Viper said.

I frowned. "Too short."

"They only need to be dick height, Kill." When I shot him a look, he sighed. "Fine. What about... Ooh. Blond quarterback looking for a tight end at my ten."

"Meh."

"The fuck does that mean? 'Meh'?"

"Not my type."

"Full, dick-sucking lips isn't your type. Right. Got it."

"Just not interested."

"You mean little Richard isn't interested."

"Jesus Christ." I rubbed my forehead, wondering why I'd thought Viper had been the best choice to join me. "Maybe don't name my dick little Richard."

Viper let out a bellowing laugh and then turned back toward the bar to order us a round of shots. When the bartender pushed a couple of who-knew-what in our direction, I threw back the alcohol before Viper even had a chance to pick his up.

"You know what your problem is?" he said. "Why you've been on the prowl for God knows how long with nothing to show for it?"

"I'm sure you're dying to tell me."

He tossed back his shot and slammed the glass back on the bar. "It's because you're in love, you dumb shit. That was your first fuck-up."

"How is falling for someone fucking up?"

"Because it means your dick isn't gonna get hard for just anyone anymore. It's fixated. Stuck on our preppie-ass manager who's decided to choose the job over you."

Fucking ouch. Viper's arrow shot straight into my chest and hurt like a bitch, but he wasn't wrong. It was the truth I didn't want to acknowledge.

"Your second fuck-up—"

"Yes, please keep going. You're making me feel so much better."

"Your *second* fuck-up," Viper said, "was pretending you didn't give a fuck about Levi the day we were talking about him. Trying to be all secretive and shit."

My jaw all but fell to the bar. "Correct me if I'm wrong, but weren't you the asshole who spent the beginning of our recording sessions acting like a total dick because you were busy pretending you and the angel were just bandmates?"

"That's different."

"How the fuck is that different?"

"Because my fuck-up wasn't in pretending I didn't *like* him. My fuck-up was in not tying the angel to the bed after I'd spent the night inside him. You see, he snuck out on me without a word in the wee hours of the morning, and *that's* why I was an asshole. Whereas you basically announced Levi was a casual fuck, which is why *you* are an—"

"I get it, I get it," I said, then threw back another gulp of bourbon. "You're really fucking annoying, you know that?"

"I've heard it a time or two."

Rolling my eyes, I gestured again for the bartender and reminded myself to leave him a good tip.

"But I'm also right."

"So what do I do now?"

Viper brought his glass to his lips and polished off the remaining contents before saying, "You grovel."

"Grovel?" I shook my head. "I already did that. He isn't interested. In fact, he pretty much told me to fuck off and kicked me out of his house."

"Really? I can't see Levi being so succinct."

"Did you really just use the word succinct? And no, he didn't use those words exactly. But it was pretty clear where he wanted me to go."

"A toasty place that's ruled by a really angry guy?"

"You're really not helping, not in even the smallest way possible."

"Look," Viper said, and swiveled in my direction. "Here's my *real* advice."

"You mean everything up until now has just been for my entertainment? I feel so special right now."

"Shut the fuck up and listen, smartass. You need to let him cool off. Levi's pissed right now, and has every right to be. He's trying to decide if you're full of shit or if he can actually trust the words coming out of your mouth. Let him calm down. Let him think about things. It's not like you don't know where to find him."

Viper had a point, and even though I hated the idea of Levi thinking anything other than amazing thoughts of me, I'd made this bed and now I was gonna have to lie in it—even if it was cold and fucking lonely right now.

About done with wallowing in my misery, I was ready to settle up with the bartender and head out when Viper's eyes rose up over my shoulder and narrowed.

"Don't look now, but jerk-off Jonny just walked in the joint with his latest piece of ass."

At the mention of The Nothing's bassist, Jonny, my spine stiffened.

"I'm assuming you didn't call him up for a good time."

The comment was one I'd usually laugh off and move on from. But after learning what a true piece of shit Jonny was from Levi, it was all I could do to stay where I was instead of going over to the fucker and taking my frustrations out on his face.

"I wouldn't call him if someone held a gun to my head and he was the only one who could save me."

Viper's eyes came back to mine. "Woooah... And here I thought I didn't like the douchebag. What'd he do to you?"

Not about to share Levi's past, I said, "He existed."

"Well, well, well, if it isn't V and his little sidekick Kill."

Not for nothing, but I was getting really sick and tired of people calling me "little" tonight.

"Your 'angel' know you're out drinking without him?" Jonny said, as he looked Viper over. "Maybe I should've called him up and seen if he wanted a little company."

"Pretty sure he'd prefer Dex's boa constrictor to you, but I'm sure you get that a lot."

"Fuck you, Viper."

"That's funny, you're the second person who's offered that tonight. But just like I told Kill, no thanks." Viper looked to me, waiting for some kind of reaction, no doubt. But I was too busy sitting with my fist clenched on the bar top, trying my hardest not to stand up, grab Jonny, and beat the ever-loving shit out of him.

"You know," Jonny said, running his eyes over me in a way that made my skin crawl. "If you're looking for someone to dip your dick in tonight, I wouldn't say no. You've always been the hot one of the group—you know, until that sexy *angel* came along."

Viper shot off his seat then and surged forward. But before he could reach Jonny, I got to my feet, grabbed hold of his arm, and halted him. That didn't, however, stop the threats from flying off Viper's tongue.

"You need to watch your fucking mouth, Jonny. Or I swear to God I'm gonna punch you in it."

"You're not gonna do that," Jonny said with a sneer, as I did my best to rein in my own temper. The last thing Levi would want was to hear how me and Viper got into a bar fight with Jonny. "What would that manager of yours think? Levi? I've heard he's a real stickler for *rules* these days."

And yeah, suddenly I didn't give a flying fuck.

Letting go of Viper, I reached out, grabbed a fistful of Jonny's black shirt, and hauled him in until we were practically nose to nose.

"I tried..." I said, my anger over the last couple days bubbling up inside me, along with a healthy dose of frustration that I had somehow wound up lumping myself in the same category as this piece of shit in Levi's eyes. "I tried to just shut my mouth while you ran yours, but you know what? Fuck you,

Jonny." I twisted my fist in his shirt, knowing I should do anything but. We were in public, there were people with phones, and this shit was about to get out of hand. "If I ever hear you say Levi's name to me, in passing, to anyone ever again? I'll make sure it's the last fucking thing you ever say. Do you hear me?"

Jonny reached up and shoved at my shoulders in an attempt to free himself. But my grip was too tight, my anger too raw, and there was no way in hell I was letting this motherfucker go until he acknowledged what I'd just said.

"Huh, looks like some habits are harder to break than others. Tell me, Killian," Jonny said with a twisted kind of grin. "Did Levi tell you he has a thing for bassists before or after he fucked you?"

My body vibrated and my blood began to boil, but it wasn't until Jonny added, "I assume that's why you're so pissed off right now. Because I had him first," that I reached my breaking point.

My fist slammed into Jonny's jaw before I even realized what I was doing.

He flew back into a table, bottles and drinks going everywhere and the table's occupants yelling and leaping to their feet. Before Jonny could lift himself up, I grabbed hold of his shirt again as my arm reared back. This time, though, someone stopped me, their grasp on my arm strong enough to pull me off.

Viper.

"Let me go." I grunted and struggled against his hold, but he wasn't having it, jerking me back from Jonny.

"He's not worth it, man. He's not fucking worth it."

Like he could talk. Viper would punch a wall if he slammed into it, and had on more than one occasion, causing Levi to run damage control.

Fuck. *Levi.*

Even with everything in my vision tinted red, as soon as Levi's face popped into my mind, I stopped fighting and let Viper walk me back to the bar.

There was no telling if anyone got a picture or a video, if there'd be any fallout from giving Jonny what he deserved, but I did know that whatever happened, Levi would have to deal with it. And that was enough to make me walk away.

Shaking my head, I headed toward the door, Viper hot on my heels as Jonny seemed to regain use of his mouth and shouted after us, "Make sure to say hi to Levi for me the next time you see him."

"Keep walking," Viper muttered from behind me as my fists began to curl.

Not worth it. No, Jonny wasn't worth the dirt on the bottom of my boots, but Levi was worth everything, and that was the only reason I was walking away now.

THIRTY-NINE

Killian

WORD TRAVELED FAST, so I really shouldn't have been surprised when Levi demanded a meeting with the entire band the day after I knocked the shit out of Jonny. I didn't know whether the others were speaking to each other after the fight over Imogen, but I knew the point of getting us all together was to work shit out—though I doubted Levi would include the two of us in that.

I made sure to have the coffee brewed strong, ready for when the guys began to trickle in. First Slade, then Halo and Viper, and it didn't escape my notice how they ended up on opposite sides of the room and didn't even speak to each other.

Leaning back against the kitchen island, I sipped my coffee and waited, not wanting to get involved in the storm still looming over the others. I had my own problems to worry about, namely what Levi would say now that he'd found out what went down last night with Jonny.

I didn't regret it. Fuck no. But I also wasn't trying to make things worse when the band seemed close to imploding as it was.

The door opened without a knock, and then Levi stepped

inside looking like a *GQ* model, if *GQ* models wore an electric-purple suit and an almost blinding yellow button-up. Even if he wasn't so damn beautiful, one thing I couldn't deny was that Levi always commanded the attention in a room, with or without the brightly colored clothes.

He scanned over the room, taking stock of who was there and who wasn't. When his gaze landed on me, he immediately moved my way, whatever he was thinking and feeling hidden behind his blank expression.

Levi grabbed a mug and then reached for the coffee pot, leaving room for a splash of milk. As he stirred the coffee, he leaned back against the counter to face me.

"Heard you had a rough night."

"Wasn't the best."

He regarded me carefully, those keen eyes not missing a thing. "So, you didn't get what you wanted and thought you'd make things better by drinking and starting a scene. In public. Where I'd have to clean up after you."

"Oh, give me a fucking break," I said, setting my mug to the side and bracing my hands on the island behind me. "You act like I went looking for trouble."

"Didn't you?"

"No."

"Then why invite Viper?"

I scrubbed a hand over my face. "Because he's my best fucking friend. Because I wanted him there, and I knew he'd be straight with me. And because—" I cut myself off there, not wanting to say that the main reason I'd invited Viper out was because he'd gone through the difficult shit with Halo and I wanted some hope that Levi and I had a chance.

Levi's face softened ever so slightly, like he knew exactly what I wasn't saying. "Look, Killian... You're the one I don't have to worry about. Please don't make me start now."

It was enough to make me feel guilty. Almost.

"I appreciate what you did," he continued, "but I don't need you to fight my battles for me."

Before I could say anything, Jagger walked in, the last piece of our dysfunctional family complete.

"We'll finish this later." Levi inclined his head toward the couches, and just like that, our conversation was closed, and it was time for why we were all really there.

Full house. Here we go.

Halo and Viper avoided eye contact with Slade and Jagger, each duo taking opposite couches while I dropped into the oversized chair and kicked my legs out onto the coffee table. Levi stayed standing at the head of the room, waiting until he had everyone's attention to begin what I was sure would be an epic lecture. Shit, we deserved it.

Levi surveyed each of us and sighed, crossing his arms. "I don't need to tell you why we're all here."

"Then why waste our time?" Viper said, reverting to being a shit, apparently.

Levi narrowed his eyes. "I don't *need* to tell you, but I'm going to anyway. Because you all can't seem to get your heads out of your asses yourselves."

I saw Halo's brow pop up, and then he put his hand over Viper's leg as if to say, *Don't start.*

"A year ago you were all treading water. You didn't even have a band anymore, not one people wanted to pay to see. Am I right?" Levi looked around, waiting for an answer, and I mumbled a yes as the others did the same. "Then what happened? You get a new singer, your album explodes, you go on a world tour for months, making more money than you've seen in years, and you've seen a shit-ton. You're riding high. You've got the world at your feet, and whatever you don't have, you know damn well I'll make happen for you."

Sitting down on the edge of an armchair, Levi placed his elbows on his knees. "I get it. Relationships are hard. Friend-

190 · LUST. HATE. LOVE.

ships are hard. Sometimes the lines get crossed, but you've got to stay focused. You want to just throw away all your success over your egos? Seriously?"

Levi turned his attention to Jagger and Slade. "You two. What the hell were you thinking? Halo's your brother and bandmate, and you went behind his back. You should've been man enough to go to him and tell him what was happening. At least have enough respect for him to do that."

"Exactly fuckin' right," Viper spat, and Levi turned in his direction.

"And you two." Levi shook his head. "Halo, your sister's business isn't *your* fucking business. I get why you're mad, and I would be too, but you've gotta let it go."

"But they're—" Halo started, but Levi put his hand up.

"In love with her. Is that right, guys?"

Slade and Jagger nodded.

"There you go. They're in love with her," Levi said. "And the two of them combined isn't nearly as traumatizing as Viper, and your sister got on board with that fairly quickly."

Viper leaned forward. "The fuck?"

"Don't even get me started on you. I'd run out of time."

I couldn't help snorting, because damn if he wasn't right about that.

Levi's gaze settled on me. "You think that's funny? You think you're any less responsible for the mess we're in?"

"Excuse me?"

"*The punch heard around the world.* That's what's all over the internet right now, courtesy of your little tantrum last night."

Little…tantrum? Was he fucking kidding?

Before I could say anything, Viper said, "And why do you think that happened in the first place, Levi? You sure as hell don't have a problem telling the rest of us what assholes we are right now, but what about you? You think you're faultless?" Viper shook his head. "Bull*shit*."

"*Viper,*" I said between gritted teeth. Was he insane? The last thing I needed was for him to air my abysmal failures to the rest of these guys. It was also—I had no doubt—the last thing Levi was in the mood to hear.

"What? It's the fucking truth." Viper got to his feet, and for a split second I wondered if this would be the second fight I was going to get into within the last twenty-four hours. "Here he is all high and mighty telling us that *our* relationships are causing problems for the band. Yet, if I'm not mistaken, *he* is the reason you landed the punch we've all wanted to for the past ten years."

Levi sat uncharacteristically quiet as I glared up at Viper. I wasn't about to get into this. Not here and not now. "Sit down."

"No," Viper said, stubborn to the end. "If Levi here wants the family to all kiss and make up, then I think it's time he admitted that he's just as much a part of this problem as the rest of us."

I got to my feet, about to haul Viper somewhere out of earshot where I could tell him to shut his fucking mouth. But as I turned in his direction, I heard, "He's right."

FORTY

Levi

———————

AT THE SOUND of my voice everyone froze, and Killian turned to see me getting to my feet.

"What did you just say?"

"Viper, he's right," I said. "Here I've been getting all up on you guys about your relationships and how they're tearing this band apart, when I've taken the one person who used to be the calming force of this chaos and turned him into—"

"Rocky Balboa?" Jagger piped up, making me look his way. "What? I saw the clip. You got to admit, Kill landed a solid hit to that fucker's face. Made me proud."

It made me want to vomit. The idea that I'd driven Killian to the point of violence or that something regarding me had? Well, that just made me want to hit something myself. Jonny, if I were being honest.

"So you two are…what, exactly?" asked Halo, who up until now had been sitting silently, watching the havoc unfold. "Friends with benefits? What? I mean, since we're all disclosing our business for everyone to have an opinion."

"We're nothing," Killian said with a finality that gutted me. But I had no one to blame for his response except myself. That had been my plan all along, right? To take us back to square one? To take us back to where we were nothing more than friends, nothing more than band manager and bassist.

Yeah, that had been the plan. It'd been a really great one, too, until I read the song he'd left behind.

Jagger slowly got to his feet then and looked between the two of us. "I don't know about that, Kill. I think I'm going to side with Viper on this one and call bullshit."

Slade bounced up to his feet too, and moved with Jagger to stand by Viper and Halo.

"Yeah. You two are full of it. What's really going on here?" Slade said as he eyed Killian.

Amazing—it was the first time in days since these guys had said shit to each other, and the first time they were all united was over whether Killian and I were...what? A couple?

I was not about to have this conversation here, and I certainly wasn't going to have it in front of the four fools grinning in mine and Killian's direction.

"What's really going on is exactly what I said: *nothing*," Killian said, and that was it. I was done.

"Killian, can I talk to you for a minute, please?"

"Uh oh," Halo said, as he looked at Viper, and I couldn't help but think how far Fallen Angel's lead singer had come. When I first arrived on the scene, he'd been shy, sweet, and much more manageable. But as he waggled his eyebrows at his boyfriend, I couldn't see any hint of that now. "I think Killian's in trouble."

Fucking Viper's influence right there.

Viper chuckled and slung an arm around Halo's shoulders. "Somehow I don't think he's gonna mind this particular spanking, Angel."

"Oh for the love of— *You*," I said, pointing at Killian, my patience now reaching its limit. "Outside, now."

As I turned on my heel and marched toward Killian's front

door, I didn't wait to see if he was following. But when the catcalls and girly *oooohs* met my ears, I knew he had to be close on my heels.

Once I was out in the hall, I paced back and forth, trying to decide what to say first. But when I heard the door click shut and turned to see Killian staring at me, all of my thoughts and well-planned arguments scattered like leaves in the wind.

God, he was beautiful, the most handsome man I'd ever seen in my life, and as I stood there trying to remember how to speak, all I could think was what a fool I'd been. What a complete and utter fool.

How long was I going to punish myself and this amazing man for something neither of us had done? Killian wasn't Jonny. He was nothing like him. He was charming, talented, and the most humble, easygoing guy I'd ever met, and somehow I'd turned him into an angry, moody version of himself. I hated myself for that.

"Well," Killian said, and his tone was bitter but also kind of...defeated. "I'm here. What did you need, Levi?"

Knowing it was now or never, I took a step toward him and sent up a silent prayer that I wasn't too late. Then I swallowed around the lump lodged in the back of my throat and said, "I read your song."

FORTY-ONE

Killian

"I READ YOUR song"?

That was what Levi had to tell me that was so important? Seriously? That was it? Heartfelt lyrics I'd written for him, and what? No reaction? Nothing but an *I know what you did last night* lashing to show for it when he'd arrived.

Man, I'd read this thing wrong. And for the first time, maybe ever, I felt like a fucking idiot. I'd put myself out there, shown this guy my heart, and he didn't give two shits.

I squared my shoulders and crossed my arms over my chest, feeling defensive and far too vulnerable. "So?" I said. Like I didn't care one way or another what he thought, when we both knew that wasn't true.

I counted on him brushing me off, telling me what he read was nice, *but...* Instead, what came out of Levi's mouth was nothing I expected.

"I was wrong."

Three seemingly simple words, but ones that were sometimes the hardest to say, and it piqued my curiosity.

"Wrong," I said, testing the word on my tongue. "What were you wrong about, Levi?"

He hesitated, staring down at my crossed arms. "So much." Before I could call him out on being vague, he continued. "I was wrong to push you away that first night back in Atlanta. Wrong to make you adhere to rules that were made because of *my* mistakes, not yours. I was wrong to compare you to a man that isn't even worth thinking about. But most of all, I was wrong to think I'd ever be able to be around you and not fall completely and utterly in love with the man you are. Because that man is the very best man I've ever met."

As Levi's words penetrated my brain and began to settle in, I uncrossed my arms and opened my mouth to respond—but nothing came out.

Was this some kind of joke? A parallel universe, where I'd stepped outside my condo and into the world I really wanted, where Levi was standing in front of me telling me he loved me? Because if it was, I'd gladly give up everything else to make *that* world my reality.

Just as I was about to tell him so, Levi took a step toward me. Then he brought a finger up and placed it over my lips, his beautiful brown eyes imploring me to let him finish.

"You scare the hell out of me, Killian Michaels." The confession was whisper soft. "From the first time we talked over the phone to the moment we met, I knew I was in trouble. And not because you were this big-shot rock god who threw his fame and fortune around like it somehow proved his dick was bigger than everyone else's in the room."

I arched an eyebrow, and Levi smirked and trailed his fingers along my jaw and down the side of my neck.

"But because you *didn't* do that. I've been in this business for years, and worked with the biggest and most badass of them all. Yet the day we met, when you had every reason to act like you had the whole world at your feet, you went out of *your* way to make *me* feel comfortable, and it only got better—or worse, if we're looking at my stubborn resolve—from there."

Levi glanced to where my shirt was open at my neck and fingered the top button, and before he could pull his hand away, I brought mine up to cover it.

"I tried to stay away," Levi whispered. "I tried to convince myself that what I was feeling would only lead to trouble. But Killian?"

It was the first time he'd actually addressed me, and this time when his thick lashes rose and his eyes met mine, I somehow found my voice long enough to say, "Yeah, Levi?"

"When I look at you, I lose my ability to think. You make me feel like I'm sixteen again and back in high school crushing on the sexy guy in the band."

I couldn't have stopped my grin if my life depended on it, because hot damn, I *loved* the idea of making the always proper, always professional Levi Walker lose his mind.

"See? That smile," he said, a faint blush coloring his cheeks. "It makes my heart race and my knees go weak. God, Killian. I never stood a chance against you. Never. I wanted you the moment we met, and fell for you not long after that. I just never thought, never dared to *believe* that you could feel the same..." Levi shook his head. "You could have anyone."

I curled my fingers around his and brought them up to my lips to press a fierce kiss there. "Maybe. But the thing is, I don't want anyone else. I want you."

FORTY-TWO

Levi

————————

I SUCKED IN a shaky breath and nodded. "I'm starting to understand that."

"*Starting* to?" Killian said, and brought my hand down to place it over his heart. "Feel that? You said I make *your* heart race. You do the exact same thing to mine. When are you going to understand, from the second you walked into my life, I was done?"

I swallowed, my fingertips digging into Killian's chest, as he reached up with his other hand to cradle my cheek.

"But you already know that, don't you, Levi?" I bit down into my lower lip, and Killian swiped his thumb over it. "How could you not? You're smart, possibly the smartest man I know. And after our first meeting, everyone else—the groupies, the casual one-nighters, the friends with benefits—they all vanished from my life. Just like I told you."

"I know," I said, my voice breathy, my heart thudding so hard that I was surprised Killian couldn't hear it.

"And why do you think I did that?"

I went to speak, but when nothing came out, Killian lowered his head and whispered in my ear, "Because you beautiful, stubborn man, I didn't want to talk to, think about, or look at anyone that wasn't you. I still don't. I love *you*, Levi. I think I always have. I was just waiting for you to walk into my life."

If it wasn't for Killian's hand holding mine, and his palm cradling my cheek, I was positive I would've melted at his feet. As it was, I was finding it increasingly difficult to think, to speak, to articulate everything my body was feeling, because never in my wildest dreams could I have imagined that Killian would be standing in his hallway telling me everything I'd ever wanted to hear.

"Killian—"

"Uh ah," he said, and trailed the back of his fingers down my cheek. "It's your turn to listen now. Your turn to understand how damn sorry I am for what I said to Viper. I didn't mean it, not any of it—"

"I know," I said, and closed my eyes as I leaned into his touch. It was time to lay this all out. If we were going to have a chance at a future together, I needed to be honest with him, and I needed to start right here. "I think, deep down, I knew at the time. I was scared. That's not easy for me to say, but this was getting more serious, and—"

"That was the easiest way to put an end to us before you thought I would?"

Wow, it was uncanny how well he knew me.

"Yes. I'm not proud of that. Or the way I acted when you came to see me at my place and apologize. You'll never know how hard it was for me to tell you to leave. But I knew if I let you back in I was going to fall all the way. I was going to wind up handing you my heart with no care as to what you ended up doing with it—and I was terrified that that would be something I couldn't recover from. Then you gave me that song…"

I caught myself as my eyes blurred and a lump formed in the back of my throat.

"Killian… That song, those words? They are some of the

most beautiful lyrics I've ever read. And to know you wrote it after our night together? Wow. I must've read them a hundred times over that night." I blinked back the tears filling my eyes and gave a halfhearted laugh. "I was a fool. I was so busy running from my past that I almost flew right by my future."

Killian let go of my hand and took hold of my face between his. "*You* are no fool. You were protecting your heart. And you didn't fly by anything. I'm standing right here, and I don't know about you, but I have a really good feeling that this future of yours...of ours, is going to be epic."

"Epic, huh?"

"When it comes to you and me, you better believe it." Killian brushed his lips over the top of mine and the sweet, almost chaste kiss made my stomach flip and my body tremble. "The reason I didn't do relationships before you was because I never wanted to promise the other person something I couldn't give—my heart. I've waited my whole life to give that over. I've waited my whole life for you. I love you, Levi."

I wound my arms around Killian's neck and pressed my lips to his cheek, then his temple, and when he wrapped his strong arms around my waist, the weight of the last few days lifted from my shoulders. I hadn't ruined this, hadn't missed my chance, hadn't missed our future.

Happiness filled my heart, my soul, my entire body, as I whispered in his ear, "I love you too," and as I stood there wrapped in Killian's embrace, I thought he'd been spot-on in how he'd described this...described us. It was certainly a story I could spin.

After all, who didn't want to read about an *epic* love affair? Certainly not me.

Epilogue

Killian
One Year Later

"YO, V, I need that plate anytime now," I called out from the patio, where I was busy flipping burgers on the grill. It was something to keep me busy so I wasn't checking my phone every five seconds for the news we'd all gathered at my—and now Levi's—place for.

Viper pushed the door open wider, an empty platter in hand. "Keep your panties on. I'm comin'."

"You want this shit burnt? Didn't think so."

Viper rolled his eyes, but held his arms out so I could transfer the burgers to the platter. When I was done, I switched off the grill and then set about cleaning the grate while it was still hot.

"You think this is gonna be enough?"

"There's twenty more patties inside, not to mention all the hot dogs. How fuckin' hungry are you?"

"I'm just sayin'. Slade and Jagger said Imogen's an eating machine lately, so I wanna make sure the rest of us get a plate."

I laughed and finished the cleanup job before following Viper inside. "Don't let her hear that or she'll kick your ass."

"Don't let her hear what? You talkin' about me?" Imogen's green eyes flashed as she swiped another chip out of the bowl on the kitchen island and loaded it down with French onion dip.

"Just how lovely you're looking lately," Viper lied smoothly, setting the platter down beside the others.

Imogen frowned. "Why would I kick your ass for that? You wouldn't be lying to me, now would you, V?"

Viper winked at me over her shoulder. "No, never."

Before Imogen really did kick his ass, I said, "Im, why don't you go put your feet up? One of your guys can make you a plate."

Imogen pointed a chip at me. "See, if Viper had said that to me, I'd think he was just trying to get rid of me, but you'd never." She popped the chip into her mouth and grabbed a handful more, dropping them onto a plate as she headed toward the living room. Before she got remotely near the couch, both Slade and Jagger popped up out of their seats, one grabbing the plate from her and the other helping her down onto the couch, a feat considering the size of her pregnant belly.

"We still on for the bet on whose baby it is?" Viper smirked my way, but didn't realize Halo was behind him until his boyfriend landed a swift hit upside his head.

"I told you to cut that shit out," Halo said, and I had to grin. He'd come a long, long way in the year since he'd found out about Imogen, Slade, and Jagger's unique threesome, and he'd only had to grow more accepting eight months ago. There'd been yet another ass beating after the baby news, but things calmed down soon after when Halo realized he'd be an uncle.

Not that he didn't shoot the guys looks at times, but he'd finally come to terms with the fact that his sister had chosen two of his bandmates to be with, and that they treated her like a queen. As long as she was happy, Halo was…tolerant. Pleasant, even.

God help them if they ever hurt her. Hell to pay would be an understatement.

"Angel, it was a joke," Viper said, turning to face Halo and planting a kiss on his boyfriend's frowning lips. "You have to admit you're curious."

Halo shrugged, not confirming or denying, but come on. He had to wonder. "Im said they've talked about it, and it doesn't matter, so…"

"One thing's for sure. That kid's gonna be seriously musically inclined," I said.

Halo's face brightened. "I've already got a miniature guitar and piano at the house, and one of those karaoke sets…"

As he continued to talk animatedly about the gifts he'd purchased that the kid wouldn't be able to use for years, movement coming from the doorway of the rehearsal studio caught my attention. A flash of fuchsia paced behind the cracked-open door, a cell phone held up to their ear.

Levi.

Even now, looking at him, knowing he was mine, made my heart beat erratically, and it had nothing to do with the information he was digging for from whomever he was speaking to. Levi in full manager mode turned me on just as much as naked Levi in our bed, and had we not had a house full of nosy bastards, I would've slipped into the rehearsal room and shown him just how hot he made me every hour of every damn day.

"Earth to Killian." Viper shook his head. "That moony face you get is enough to make me gag. Can we eat now before I start dry heaving?"

Halo snorted. "You are such a hypocrite, you know that?"

"You callin' me out, Angel?"

"Damn right I am. Kill's not the only one who gets that look on his face." Halo placed his mouth by Viper's ear and whispered something that had Viper grabbing two handfuls of Halo's ass, like he was ready to haul him away.

Thank God Levi chose that moment to throw open the rehearsal room door, sending it slamming back into the stopper with a loud noise that had everyone's attention turning his way.

Oh shit. The look on his face was unreadable as ever, which meant the news could be good…or it could spell a change for Fallen Angel.

Levi scanned the room, stopping when he saw me. Then he smiled. "Looks like the food's ready. Let's eat."

Silence engulfed the space as we all stared at Levi, who made his way to the kitchen and picked up a plate like we weren't all dying to hear what he wasn't saying.

Stacking his plate with macaroni salad and baked beans, Levi ignored the tension in the air and moved on down the line. Hamburger bun, cheese, lettuce, tomato. As he reached for one of the patties, I grabbed his arm.

Levi looked down at the hold I had on him, and then his eyes flicked to where I was anxiously spinning the platinum band on my left hand with my thumb. He reached for my hand, running his fingers over my knuckles and the ring, and then he softly kissed my lips.

"Don't worry," he said, and then he let go of me and went back to building his hamburger.

The knots in my stomach loosened slightly, but I knew they wouldn't completely go away until I knew for sure how things were going.

"You've gotta be fucking kidding me," Jagger said, shooting to his feet, his hands on his hips. "Spill it, man."

Slade nodded, but didn't move from Imogen's side. "Just tell us already."

"Yeah, so we know whether to celebrate or throw ourselves off the fuckin' balcony," Viper cracked, and then he let out an "oof" and a laugh as Halo's elbow rammed into his side.

I didn't often use my and Levi's relationship as leverage in the band, since, despite everything, Levi still wanted to maintain some sense of a professional line, but in this case, I was going to work him to my advantage.

As Levi set his plate down on the dining table, I moved around the island, stopping behind him and wrapping my arms around his waist.

"Babe?" I said, my lips on his neck sending a shiver through him that had my cock stiffening in an instant. *Not now*, I thought, as Levi covered my hands where they rested on his stomach. The sunlight pouring in caused the matching platinum band on his hand to gleam, and I relished the sight, though I'd had three months to get used to it.

Husband. Even now I had to pinch myself, because the word seemed so foreign and yet so important at the same time.

I kissed Levi's neck softly. "I think you're going to have a riot on your hands if you put this off any longer."

"Including yourself in that?"

"Damn right I am. You're killing me here." I pushed my hips into his ass so he could feel my growing erection. "In all the ways."

Levi's chest rumbled with laughter, and then he spun around to face me. His eyes glinted with amusement, and I couldn't help myself. I had to have a taste.

As always, Levi's mouth opened to mine immediately, and I took my time, teasing his tongue, savoring the way his lips against mine felt so right. They always had.

Like home.

206 • LUST. HATE. LOVE.

"Jesus Christ, I know you're newlyweds, but can you give it a fucking rest? Some of us want to eat," Viper grumbled, and Levi pushed me away. The hint of a smile on his face told me he wasn't done with me yet, but it would have to wait.

For now.

Levi cleared his throat and stepped around me, every eye in the house focused completely on him. "I guess you want to know how the album's doing."

"No shit," Imogen said, causing both her guys to chuckle.

"Fair enough," Levi said. "I just got off the phone with a contact of mine who's got the early numbers, and I feel like we need to talk."

My stomach dropped. *We need to talk* was never something good, and I could see the instant worry on the rest of the guys' faces as well. *Shit.*

Levi took a deep breath and let it out slowly. "Guys...when your *Corruption* album hit, it was a crazy time. You were the hot new band with a killer new lead singer, and the songs were dirty, edgy. Different. A million albums sold in a week is an unheard-of number for anyone anymore."

The knots in my stomach tightened. Levi had told me not to worry. *Not to worry?* This little chat wasn't leading anywhere good. I bit down on the inside of my cheek to resist the urge to vomit.

Levi continued, "With this new album, you really went for it, and you should be damn proud. For a rock band to maintain that level of grit while moving forward, pouring out love songs better than any power ballad I've ever heard? It shouldn't work. But somehow, the combination of the five of you *makes* it work. It's important that your music reflects what's going on in your life, and *Surrender* does that. I'm proud to stand by you on this album."

"Oh my God," Halo said, burying his head in Viper's back. "Just say it already."

Levi straightened. "Early numbers are reporting that *Surrender* sold three million copies in its first week."

The room went dead silent, no one even breathing as we took in that information. It was a long time, minutes, before someone spoke.

"I think I heard you wrong," Viper said. "Did you say… three million copies?"

Levi's face broke into a huge grin. "Yes. Yes, I fucking did."

Halo's jaw dropped. "Holy shit. Holy *shit*."

As the number finally penetrated our brains, shouts of disbelief and celebration rang out, all while I stood there, completely numb.

"Hey." Levi moved in front of me, taking my face in his hand. "Did you hear what I said?"

I nodded.

"In shock?"

I nodded again, and Levi laughed, throwing his arms around me as everyone else in the room went nuts. All I could manage to do was hug Levi back, wrapping my arms so tight around his waist that I wondered for a moment how he managed to breathe.

"Oh my God," I said, repeating it over and over as Levi held me tight. It didn't seem possible that we'd not only reached *Corruption*'s first week sales, but surpassed it by a huge margin. And to have done it with all of us contributing, and with songs I'd written about the very man in my arms.

Fuck me, that felt good.

"You happy?" Levi pulled back so he could look at me, that brilliant smile on his face lighting me up inside.

Happy? There needed to be another word for happy, because it didn't seem like a big enough expression for what I felt. It'd taken so many years to find what I'd needed to make me whole, and between finding the man I never knew to dream for and the current iteration of Fallen Angel, I couldn't imagine anything I could want more.

It was overwhelming and indescribable, and never in my wildest dreams had I thought love could be this way.

Life, now and forever, with the man in my arms, would always be...perfect.

Special Thanks

We've had such an amazing time writing these Fallen Angel guys, and we're thrilled with how much you've told us you love Killian & Levi too. Thank you so much for spending time with our guys!

We'd like to thank the following talented humans for helping us bring LUST. HATE. LOVE. to life:
- Hang Le for the gorgeous Fallen Angel Series covers, banners, and teasers
- Arran for an always entertaining edit
- Charlie David for bringing these sexy men to life on audio
- Rafa Catala Photography for the killer cover photo
- Our cover model for Lust. Hate. Love - Fabián Castro

A huge thank you to the bloggers who support our work by taking time out of their busy lives to share our releases. You're the real rock stars. <3

Finally, if you're reading this, we'd also like to thank YOU for picking up our Fallen Angel series. We're so grateful to be able to write these stories in our head for a living, and that is only possible with your continued support. A million thank you's and big bear hugs.

xoxoxox,

Brooke & Ella

About Ella Frank

If you'd like to get to know Ella better, you can find her getting up to all kinds of shenanigans at:

The Naughty Umbrella

And if you would like to talk with other readers who love Robbie, Julien & Priest, you can find them **HERE** at *Ella Frank's Temptation Series Facebook Group.*

Ella Frank is the *USA Today* Bestselling author of the Temptation series, including Try, Take, and Trust and is the co-author of the fan-favorite contemporary romance, Sex Addict. Her Exquisite series has been praised as "scorching hot!" and "enticingly sexy!"

Some of her favorite authors include Tiffany Reisz, Kresley Cole, Riley Hart, J.R. Ward, Erika Wilde, Gena Showalter, and Carly Philips.

Want to stay up to date with all things Ella? You can sign up here to join her newsletter

About Brooke Blaine

About Brooke

Brooke Blaine is a *USA Today* Bestselling Author of contemporary and LGBT romance that ranges from comedy to suspense to erotic. The latter has scarred her conservative Southern family for life, bless their hearts.

If you'd like to get in touch with her, she's easy to find - just keep an ear out for the Rick Astley ringtone that's dominated her cell phone for years. Or you can reach her at www.Brooke-Blaine.com.

Brooke's Links
Brooke's Newsletter
Brooke & Ella's Naughty Umbrella

www.BrookeBlaine.com
brooke@brookeblaine.com